Matched with Her Fake Fiance

BRITNEY M. MILLS

To Max,
For laughing with me and giving me a future that's better than the
dream.

CHAPTER 1
Dani

Friday nights don't have the same excitement or relief they did in college. Which, for me, was less than a month ago. I could end the week knowing life would be okay even if I didn't do so well on my calculus test. I'd go out with the girls and my ex-boyfriend, Clay, and enjoy every minute of whatever we did, because I knew I had time before I "officially grew up."

Adult things make me want to find the customer service line and cancel my subscription. Can't there be an "I didn't learn all I needed to in my teenager-hood" lane that will allow me to go back and relearn all the things I forgot? A few more months, even a year or two should do it.

I wait outside The Riptide, a fun little restaurant in downtown Boston I've always wanted to try. And my date is already ten minutes late.

That's another thing about college. For all except six months of my undergraduate degree, I had a boyfriend.

Clay and I started dating in high school. I'd been duped into thinking the end of college would mean he'd be down on one knee holding out an engagement ring of any size or shape, and that we'd ride off into the sunset with a happily ever after. We came back after Christmas break of our senior year, and he gave me the sob story.

"It's me, not you."

Which I believed until I saw him walking down the road in front of my apartment building, holding hands with my mortal enemy. If you buy the newest edition of the dictionary, you might see my photo under the term 'heartbroken.'

I never had to think about meeting guys back then because I already found him. And now I was constantly in the up and down sea of trying to connect with someone who likes me back. I've gone on twelve first dates since then, but my date tonight counts as number three with the same guy. Progress is progress, right?

Okay, so Cameron is my first attempt at a relationship since the breakup. And attempt is the real descriptive word because there is no talking long-term with the guy. If I ask him what he's doing tomorrow, we'll end up in a conversation about how he broke his arm in elementary school and it's left him with some emotional trauma.

The man can dodge a question like my younger sister, Harper. Anytime our mom asks her something, she launches into a crazy long discussion that pacifies her audience and makes us forget the original query.

To be honest, I don't see a future with the guy. Now I'm wondering why I've been standing here so long, allowing the irritation to fester. Maybe it's the fact that he doesn't respect me or my time.

Adulting and planning a future. It's like a bad drink.

Cameron and I met on a cruise a couple weeks ago when my brother, Landon invited me. That was back when he was still sad and single.

I shake my head. I've missed my chance to play that as a nickname of sorts. Landon married one of the most amazing people on the planet, his long-time girlfriend and former fiancé (twice), Rachelle. And I'm pretty sure they are #couplegoals now that they've bridged a few hurdles.

I glance toward the street, watching as an older couple gets into a cab. The man holds the woman's purse over one arm and her hand with his other, helping her slide in through the door.

My chest squeezes and the familiar ache swoops in.

Is it too much to ask for a future with that? The caring, sweetness of it all.

Trying to date now is like repeatedly banging my head against the wall and hoping for a different result.

Back to Cameron. Is it sad that I'm bored just thinking about him? It might be time to start letting things just be after tonight. If he ever gets here.

Yep, that's what I'm doing. I'll just delete his number from my phone.

I'm a confident, smart woman in Boston, working to get over the betrayal of my ex-boyfriend. I think that's a good start at an affirmation. It could use some work, but that will have to come later.

"Danielle," a voice says from behind me. I turn to see Amber Dettling, the woman who'd stolen my ex-boyfriend all those months before. A loud groan rumbles through me and I'm wishing I'd either gone inside sooner or had left altogether.

"Amber," I say through clenched teeth.

"I didn't think I'd see you again after graduation. Ever." She walks closer and gives me a good up and down glare.

Amber and I had been assigned a research assignment in one of our courses last fall. She'd done nothing for it and struggled through our presentation after promising to pay for my books the next semester if I'd give her my notes. Which I didn't do. Cue the animosity there. She received a zero and I got an A.

Triumph at everything working out how I wanted was quickly replaced with tears and frustration as I'd had to watch her and Clay make out every time I was near.

"You know what, Amber? I was kind of hoping the same thing." I glance down the sidewalk in search of Cameron.

Apparently, I have a type and it's names that start with C.

My eyes catch on a man striding toward us. His broad shoulders are accentuated by his suit, and when my gaze drifts up to his face, I feel like the heart eyes emoji.

"Did you and Clay get back together?" Amber says, pulling my attention back to her face. Her lips turn up into the perfect pout, her lipstick a dark shade of red. Her dress is stunning, the emerald color of the gems enhancing her skin tone. And now I feel like an old-time governess in my A-line tulle skirt and homemade jewelry from one of my new roommates. My blouse is the newest thing I've bought in the past four years, but it's almost like a wilted flower next to Amber.

I shake my head. "No, that ship sailed, far, far away." Why can't I think of a better comeback line when I need it? If only I had caught onto all the red flags sooner in our five-and-a-half-year relationship. I'm in a good place now, as long as I keep moving forward.

"What about you? Did you come here by yourself?" My tone is snippy, and I need to rein in the sarcasm before it goes full tilt. No need to ruin a Friday night over her ridiculous antics.

The man I ogled not moments before stops next to her, his eyebrows pinched together. "Is there something wrong, Amber?"

Of course the hot guy is with her.

She gives him a coy smile and shakes her head, her perfect curls hardly moving. What does she use in her hair? Maybe it would help my slightly frizzy locks make it through this humid Boston summer.

"No, Danielle here graduated with me this past spring."

I grit my teeth in an attempt to be civil. Amber knows my dislike of my full name and yet she tries to use it at every turn. Boston may be a big city, but apparently not big enough to avoid my enemies.

The man standing next to her turns to me and nods, giving me a forced smile. "Congratulations on your graduation." He turns back to her and asks, "Did you get a table?"

Amber's nose turns up and she says, "Can't we go to Trey's party, Miles? I'm sure there will be plenty of food there." Her attention focuses on me once again and she says, "Sorry to be so rude. This is Miles Clark, heir to the Clark Medical Group."

Rude my behind. She's just trying to rub it in that she's got an heir at her side, while I'm waiting on someone who hasn't even called to tell me he'd be late. It's a well-known common courtesy.

The man shakes his head. "You don't have to introduce me to everyone like that." He steps forward with his hand outstretched. "I'm just Miles."

I take his hand and shake it a bit. His hand is strong and large, nearly dwarfing mine. There are no thick calluses, which is different from my typical dates. Not that I even have a chance to date him. Just another reason I wasn't meant for the upper crust of society.

"Well, Just Miles. I'm—"

"Dani," a familiar voice calls, and I turn to see Cameron coming up the walk. "Sorry I'm late. I couldn't find parking."

I paste on a smile and shake my head. "I told you parking is hard to find around here." It's nearly impossible to find parking anywhere in Boston. It's the reason I only use my car when I'm heading out of the city completely.

Cameron glances up and his face goes all soft, but I realize he's not looking at me. "Hey," he says.

"Hello," Amber says. "Oh, Danielle, were you able to find a boyfriend after Clay dumped you? That's so sweet." The fake tone in her voice only grates on my nerves further.

"This is—" I begin before Cameron cuts me off.

"We're not together," he says. I whirl around with a wide-eyed expression.

"We're on a date," I say through clenched teeth.

Something passes over Cameron's face and I can't quite describe it. Maybe it would be better if I go home now. Cut my losses and enjoy a chick flick with my roommate, Kenzie.

"Isn't that great?" Amber says, and I'm sure I could die right here. "Why don't you sit with us?"

"I'm sure they want to sit by themselves, Amber," Miles says, moving one hand up to straighten his tie.

I nod. "Yeah, we'll see you n—"

"That would be great. The more, the merrier," Cameron says. He walks over and opens the door for Amber and Miles. He follows close behind, letting the door shut before I've moved from my spot on the sidewalk.

I wave to no one and say, "Don't worry about me."

They're already walking toward one side of the dim restaurant. Now I'm wishing we'd gone to a sports bar or something. That would be easier than this romantic vibe.

Cameron is practically salivating over Amber like she's some kind of treat as he waves for me to scoot into the booth.

My mom's voice echoes in my head, "Remember to think of the positive. You can change a situation by the change in your attitude."

This won't be as bad as being alone with Cameron. Maybe he'll keep his phone put away this time.

The last time we went out for dinner, he'd propped it up against his drink glass because his favorite team was playing.

I'm all for sports, but there's a time and place for it.

The server comes to take our drink orders and leaves. I look over the menu.

"Anyone have suggestions on what to get here?" I ask. I don't have a ton of money to go out all that often, and so when I do, it's usually to the same places where I get the same dependable meal time and time again. That way I know I won't be disappointed.

"Any of the steaks are good," Miles says, his menu already closed. He glances around the restaurant, as if he's not happy sitting next to the window. It isn't my favorite place either, but Cameron had finally acknowledged me when we'd arrived at the table so I didn't bother to say anything.

6

"I think I'll get the ribeye," Cameron says. As I glance at the price next to the description, I try to keep a straight face. There have been months where I've been able to do most of my grocery shopping for that price.

Cameron and I paid for ourselves the last time we went out, and I'm now hoping that's the agreement again. All the cons keep adding up as I think about why in the world I'd accepted his invitation for dinner tonight.

His knee jabs into my thigh and I wince. "What happened?"

"Sorry, I got my, uh, shoe stuck on the legs of the table." He doesn't even look at me while apologizing.

I go down the list of food items, searching the prices on each. I don't get paid until next week and my checking account is dangerously low as it is. The smallest steak comes with two sides and some rolls. I can splurge on that since I don't want to look like a peasant in front of Amber. I have chips at home if I get hungry later.

The server returns with our drinks and the orders begin. "I'll get the large house salad, with raspberry vinaigrette on the side," Amber says.

Miles orders steak, at least that's what I think it is because there are a lot of foreign words and descriptions in there. Cameron gets his ribeye, only he says "rabbi" and it's kind of hard to keep a straight face.

Once I give my order to the server, Amber announces she's heading to the restroom to "freshen up."

A minute of silence passes as the buzz around us is the only sound. "I need to run to the bathroom as well," Cameron says, ducking out of the booth.

Awesome. This is just what I want to do on a Friday night. Sit across from a stranger in awkward silence.

"How did you meet Amber?" I ask, curious as to their connection.

"At a function our mothers worked on a few months ago. I'd

just broken up with a long-time girlfriend and she hinted at going on a date."

A man who could take a hint? I've never found one of these out in the wild before.

"What about you and Carter?" Miles asks, twisting the straw paper around his finger.

I'm mid-sip of my water and feel it go up my nose. At least he's amusing. "Cameron? We met on a cruise my brother invited me on." I realize that sounds awkward and start waving my hands in the air. "I mean, my brother's company invited him on the trip and allowed him to bring someone, which was me. I helped him get back together with his ex-fiancée and hung out with Cameron here and there."

Miles nods, leaning forward so his arms are on the table. I didn't realize he's as large as he is, but I run a finger under my collar, pulling it out a bit as the intimidation sets in.

"Interesting. What is it you do, Danielle?"

I shake my head and say, "It's Dani. Please call me Dani."

"Okay, Dani." The words sound foreign on his lips, but one side turns up in a half-smile.

"I am a Development Officer up at Boston University."

"And what does a development officer typically do?" His hands are together, and a bead of sweat runs down my back. The interrogation of the first date has begun and I'm the worst at these. He isn't my date, but it feels awfully close to one.

Why didn't I stay home?

I smile, doing my best to organize my thoughts and quickly. Where is Cameron?

"So I just started last week, but the job description is working on parties and mixers to help get alumni to come back and support the school while also helping them make connections with one another."

Miles smiles, only a fraction bigger than the half-smirk I saw a few moments ago, but the man is hitting the attractive meter inside me, and I have to tamp that down. I'm sitting here on a date with another guy and Miles is way out of my league.

"That's interesting. I went to Boston University myself."

I smile, happy to find former Terriers. It might help my job in the future. "It's a good school. I attended Northeastern, but Boston University has been good to me so far." For the six days I've been there.

We fall back into silence, and I glance toward the bathrooms. From our table, I have an almost straight-line shot to see the hallway of them, although it's dark. A man walks down and opens the men's room, the light from it shining into the hall and revealing a certain green-shaded dress. Why would Amber have gone into the men's room?

My heart rate picks up and I scoot out of the booth. "I'm going to go see where our dates are," I say, hoping it's just a trick of the lights or my imagination taking over.

I'm near the hallway when the man who'd gone in before walks out and there is a clear shot of Amber and Cameron furiously making out.

"Seriously?" I say, and it must've been loud enough for them to hear because they break apart and glance out the door. Gagging, I turn around, taking two large steps before I'm stopped by a couple servers with their arms loaded down with orders.

Of all the places to make out, the men's restroom? So many germs, and guys are just gross most of the time.

"Dani, this isn't what it looks like," Cameron says, walking over to me.

"Oh really? What was it like? Because from my angle, your lips were fused to hers." My voice goes a bit higher as I point to Amber, who's wiping around her lips with her fingers.

I turn to head back to the table but slam into the large form of Miles.

"What's going on?" he asks in his deep voice.

I turn to slip past them while saying, "Ask them. I'm done."

It's only a few more steps to the table, but the servers are now putting our food down. I see our server and ask, "Can I pay for my food now? And a box? I'll take it to go."

"Of course," the woman says, "I just need to deliver this plate to table five and I'll come back with your box."

I try to hand her my card, but she moves away too quickly.

There's a scuffle behind me, but I can't even turn to look, I'm so frustrated with myself. I saw this coming, all the signs and the irritation with Cameron.

Why is it so hard to cut ties and be done?

Because I'd been with Clay for over five years. And it was like running an uphill marathon. Everyone says that relationships are work, but at the rate I'm going, I'm not sure I'll ever make it to the crest of the hill I've labeled Fiancé Status.

"It's not a big deal, man. There's chemistry between the two of us." Cameron is such an idiot.

Footsteps approach and I hear him call out, "Dani."

Maybe my brain shorts out, but I grab Cameron's glass of Dr Pepper and start throwing it before I've turned all the way around. And as the liquid flies through the air, on its way to hitting Miles and his probably expensive suit coat, I'm wishing for a way to take it all back.

The slow motion of it all ends quickly as time goes back to its normal pace. The restaurant is silent and all eyes are turned toward us.

"Miles, I'm so, so sorry. I thought you were—"

He raises his hand, swatting at some of the sticky liquid on his suit coat. "It's fine."

I turn and grab the stack of napkins from the table, handing them to him. With slow, measured strokes, he works down the front of his suit coat. I've been able to tune Cameron and Amber out until now.

"Why are you touching him?" Amber says defensively. In my usually helpful nature, I must've kept a couple napkins as I'm dabbing Miles's arm dry.

"Because I made a mess," I say. "But then again, so did you."

We enter a stare off for several seconds before she brushes her curls over her shoulder.

"You are a walking disaster," Amber says. I ignore her to turn around. Digging into my purse, I find the business cards I'd stuck in there yesterday.

"Here is my card," I say, stretching out my hand to Miles. "Please call me with the price of the dry cleaning and I'll pay it. Or I can pick up the suit and take it to the dry cleaners for you."

Miles's slight smile appears again, and he shakes his head. "That won't be necessary. I can clean a suit."

"But I'm the one who ruined it." In a bold move, I step forward and tuck the card into the front pocket of his coat, patting it a couple times as if he needs to keep it safe. It's about the only place the sticky dark liquid isn't still clinging to.

It's only then that I glance behind him to see no evidence of Amber or Cameron.

"Where did they go?" I ask, waving behind him.

"Probably to hook up somewhere else." Miles sits down and pulls the napkin down onto his lap.

I frown, trying to put the scene all together. "You're going to eat after all that? What about the stickiness?" I glance over at his suit and cringe.

He shrugs. "Why not? I was planning on breaking up with Amber soon anyway. She just made it that much easier for me. And my food is here. Might as well eat."

His nonchalance to the whole ordeal has me wondering if I've missed an important step in life. Is it really okay not to spiral downward after a breakup? Even if the relationship is short-lived?

The server comes back with a box and the ticket.

"Thank you." I take the box and place it next to my plate. I have to hunt for my card again, finding it on the floor under the table. I must've dropped it when I'd decided to throw a beverage. By the time I glance up, our server is gone.

"I just wanted to pay for this and go home," I mumble.

Miles shakes his head. "You might as well eat it now. It won't be as good once you make it home."

He's probably right. The smell of the food makes my stomach rumble and I pick up my fork, deciding I'll eat a little bit until our server appears again.

And here I sit, on a pseudo-blind date.

Not how I thought tonight would turn out.

CHAPTER 2

Miles

My life has always been strange, but I never thought I'd be the victim of a Dr Pepper drive-by. Even after I made it home, and showered, I kept finding sticky spots just about everywhere. Getting soda out of my hair was the worst.

I've already dropped off the suit at the dry cleaners the next day and smile on my way to watch one of my best friends play hockey for the Boston Breeze.

The woman last night had spunk. I can't help but laugh as I think about it. She probably didn't know who I was, but then again, she hadn't said anything when Amber announced my name and rank, as though we were in a period drama.

And yet, she still offered to pay the dry cleaning bill. I can't say that's ever happened to me before.

It had taken stealth to hand the server my card while she'd been rooting around under the table to retrieve hers. We'd even had a substantial conversation about things besides fashion and money before I had to box up her date's food and tell her the bill had already been taken care of.

The fact she turned down the salad makes me like her even

BRITNEY M. MILLS

more. Don't get me wrong, I enjoy a good salad from time to time. I've just been out with women who take two bites and say they're full. Maybe I've just been striking out when it comes to the right woman. If only there was a surefire way to figure out the best type for me, I'd be all over it.

Most women only see me for dollar signs since my family's company hit the billion-dollar range. It gets old not being able to trust people. If only everyone could be as honest as Dani was last night. She didn't treat me different than the rest of the people there, and she was polite to the server, which is new territory for my dates. Not that it was a date, but it had the ambience of one.

At the end of the night, she said goodbye and headed toward the train. I couldn't believe she'd turned down my offer to drop her off, but it was just one more reason why I was intrigued by her. At least I didn't have to put up with Amber's antics for one more night.

Best break-up ever.

I come back to the present and walk into the suite near the corner of the arena for the Breeze. One of my good friends from high school, Trey Hatch, was drafted by the Chicago Tornadoes a year out of high school. After five seasons there, he'd been traded up to the Breeze the year before. Having him back completed our friend group.

My two other good friends, Jack and Spencer, are here. Spence was once a child star who's been trying to figure out what to do with his life ever since. He's worked on several voice-over jobs for a few animated films that have come out recently.

And Jack is the same old Jack, always joking and giving everyone a hard time. He and Trey are the most alike in that way. If it was possible, he could make sarcasm his day job. He went against his mother's wishes and became a vet, finishing two years ago.

"Look who decided to show up," Jack says, holding out his hand for a high five. Well, it's more of a morphed form that takes about ten seconds instead of one. We came up with it when we were roommates in college, and the routine stuck.

"How's it going, guys?" I say, nodding to the others. We're not the only ones in the room, but it's nice to see the game from the box instead of in the uncomfortable chairs. I know I shouldn't complain, but supporting a friend doesn't have to be physically uncomfortable.

I glance around the room, smiling at Mrs. Hatch, Trey's mom. She's in a full-out, arms waving conversation with another couple I don't recognize. Two others, employees from Clark Medical, are here and it looks like they're chatting with three investors we've been trying to get to our side.

"Dude, you missed it," Spencer says, waving a can of Dr Pepper in the air. I take a step or two away from him, not wanting to go through the showering process like last night. "Carson Carver is on fire tonight. The Breeze won the face-off and he took it down and scored within the first fifteen seconds."

"How is Trey doing?" I ask. Trey works in the same capacity as Carson Carver, and while they are competition with each other technically, Trey said Carson is an awesome guy, one who took Trey under his wing and helped him get through the first couple weeks of hockey with the team.

"He's doing pretty well out there," Spencer says. "I mean, we're only five minutes into the game."

"I still can't believe we beat you here. What brings you in late?" Jack asks. "You're always on time or thirty minutes early to everything."

I laugh, nodding. It's true. I played lacrosse growing up and my coach had drilled it into me that being early was the most respectful thing to do. My mother was just grateful that I finally learned after years of nagging me about how it looks to other people.

"I had to drop off a suit to the cleaners because I got Dr Pepper all over it."

That got the guys' attention. "I thought you were anti-soda in general right now." Jack is holding his arms out at his sides with a smirk.

"I didn't say I was the one drinking it," I say, matching his pose.

"Then what the heck happened?" Spencer asks. He moves his hands so fast that the drink spills over and I flinch back. Great, am I going to have PTSD from Dr Pepper?

We sit down in the few chairs facing the ice and I tell them all about my adventures of last night. I know I'm telling the story right when they almost miss out on the action down on the rink and laugh at certain points.

"I'm just glad you got rid of Amber," Jack says. "She was a nightmare."

Spencer nods. "You need to find a better girl and not just the next rebound."

"Yeah, just because Tanya is an idiot doesn't mean you need to go throw your life away with the first chick who throws herself at you." Jack is focused on the play below, but his teeth grind as his mind is somewhere else.

I wait as they continue to spew their thoughts. It's always interesting to know exactly how they've been feeling. I just wish it wasn't after the fact.

"You could've told me this while I was going out with Amber, right?" I say.

"We didn't want to hurt you, man," Spencer says, slapping me on the back.

I roll my eyes. "Since when have I ever been hurt about your feedback?"

At the same time, they both say, "Tanya."

"Touché."

They're right about that one. My ex-girlfriend, almost ex-fiancée, Tanya and I met at an event our mothers had organized almost three years ago. Jack, Spencer, and Trey had all given warnings about her but I was too blind to see it. Things had been going well, until she decided to take a job in New York without telling me. It wasn't until I came by her apartment as the movers were packing everything into a truck that the truth came out.

We tried the long-distance thing for a couple months. Correction: I tried the long-distance thing. She only answered one of my phone calls and that was to tell me to stop calling.

It took a while for me to come to terms with the breakup, but I don't think my mom has recovered. Tanya comes from Boston elite and our union would've been the cherry on top of my mother's successful ventures.

"To be honest, I dated Amber to get back at my mom. She's been pressuring me to settle down and has even tried to set things back up with Tanya. So while Amber wasn't the best choice, she at least deterred my mother from having those conversations every time we're at the office."

Jack's eyes narrow, studying me. "Really? Your mom needs to retire or go on a vacation somewhere."

"As much as I want her to retire, then she'd have full-time nagging capabilities," I say, knowing my mother's retirement would only happen if she is hospitalized or has amnesia. "Amber and I have been going out for like three weeks. It's not like it was that long."

"So, what about Dr Pepper girl? Was she hot?" Spencer asks. Leave it to him to go straight for the looks.

"I'm not in a place to be dating anyone right now," I say, shrugging it off. If only my brain didn't conjure a picture of Dani. She laughed at all my quippy comments and I'd been comfortable. Happy even.

"He's got a point," Jack says, pointing to Spencer. "If you're trying to get your mom off your back, why not go out with that girl? It sounds like you had some kind of connection."

Why not? Probably because rejection hurts anyway it comes, and I'd rather not be the fool twice. Tanya's brush-off still stabs at me every once in a while and I'm already seven months out.

"I don't know, guys." I try to think of another topic of

conversation. Maybe being with someone isn't in the cards for me.

"You could always find a girl and fake date." Spencer and I turn to Jack. He's officially lost his mind.

"Why would anyone fake date?" Spencer says, standing up to go get a drink from the small refrigerator. There's action out on the ice and I see Trey skating away from the opposing team for a break away.

"Come on, Trey!" we all yell. He takes a shot, but it hits the left post. The puck ricochets off and heads away from the goal.

"People fake date all the time. Haven't you seen any movies with that as a plot?" Jack asks. Spencer and I glance at each other and then back at Jack, surprised by his admission.

I shake my head. "No, I haven't. And even if it's in a movie, that doesn't mean real people negotiate this every day. I'm already having a hard time keeping a real relationship going. What good would a fake one be?"

"Because you're a celebrity, man," Jack says. "Sometimes it's nice to have someone on your arm to get through all those crappy events you have to go to."

I lean back, taking in his expression. "You've done it, haven't you? You've fake dated."

He shrugs. "Yeah, when I was younger. It was easier to keep pretending I was with Ashley Lewis than admit we broke up. And neither of us was interested in dating other people at the time."

Spencer's jaw nearly hits the floor. "You didn't tell us about that."

"I didn't meet you all until we'd officially broken up, from fake dating as well." Jack and I had been assigned roommates freshman year at BU and then roommates every year after. Even with that history, I'm still surprised he hasn't talked about this before.

I shake my head. "There's no way I can fake date anyone. I don't have someone who I've been friends with forever who'd do that for me."

Jack grins, and I usually regret whatever he says after that appears. "You don't have to have been childhood friends forever to fake date. Catch up with the times, boys. It's called Dating Apps. They are the magic wand to fix all your needs."

"No way," I say. "Not a chance. If a woman joins a dating app, it usually means she wants to have something come of the relationship. Like wedding bells."

"Wifey status," Spencer says, chuckling.

And after all that happened between me and Tanya, I'm not sure I ever want to go down that road again.

"You have to think logically," Jack continues. "Sure, there are plenty who want a ring on their finger, but there are a lot who've been hurt just like we have. So why not use the truth to explain all that?"

I laugh, shaking my head. "You? Truthful to women? That would be a first."

Jack raises his hands in defense. "Hear me out. I've never lied to a woman about anything, I've just omitted certain things from our conversations."

"Also known as a lie of omission," I say, raising an eyebrow.

"Whatever, Señor Perfect. I'm just saying this could be a possibility." Jack opens his phone and starts tapping away. I get lost in the hockey game before his questions begin.

"What is your favorite movie?"

I turn to him, scrunching my nose. "I've told you a million times that James Bond is the ultimate series."

"Which actor though?" Spencer asks, pausing with a forkful of pulled pork in front of his face. The food from here is usually amazing, but I'm not feeling barbecue at the moment.

I grin. "Daniel Craig for sure. And that last release was epic."

Jack waves a hand in the air and says, "Hold on there, Miles. You're starting to sound like a wannabe eighteen-year-old again."

I shake my head. "There isn't a better word for it. All the storylines combine to perfectly tie off all the ends. It was better than I could've imagined."

"The guy died," Spencer says, acting as though I'm a horrible person for that.

Jack glances down at his phone again. "What about your bucket list travel destination?"

Instead of answering the question, I reach over and take his phone. "What are you looking at?" I focus on the screen and see a logo at the top.

Love, Austen Matchmaking.

"Are you kidding me? You're signing me up for a dating app? That's a no."

Taking in a deep breath, Jack says, "Again, fake relationship. But you do have to fill in all the questions to apparently match up with women in the system."

I frown. "That sounds a lot like I'm signing up for a trust package that I will eventually break because I'm not ready for a relationship." I don't realize how loud my voice is getting until all the other eyes in the suite are on me. Irritation gets the best of me, and I slide my elbows down to my knees, trying to focus on the play out on the ice.

"Oh, but Miles," a voice says from behind me. I turn and see Trey's mother grinning. "There are so many amazing women I could set you up with. Why don't you come over this week and we can work on finding you someone great?"

My smile is wooden, but I'm just trying to save face. "If you're making your roast beef, Mrs. Hatch, I'll be over to help you eat it."

She laughs and I join in. She's one person I can always joke with, someone who doesn't take me as seriously as my mother or the other owners of Clark Medical Group.

"Sounds good. Jack and Spence, you're both invited too. Maybe we can get Trey to find a nice girl as well."

We all give her fake smiles before she turns to talk with some other ladies in the suite.

"Let me see that," I say. I lean over Jack's phone and start thumbing through the multiple questions. "If she's jumping on the setting-up-dates bandwagon, I might as well take this into my own hands."

Jack takes a sip of his soda and nods. "If she's playing matchmaker, we might all need that app."

CHAPTER 3

Dani

"Time for another?" Kenzie asks from the chair next
to me.

"Movie or tub of ice cream?" I ask, half-laughing,
half-crying at the idea. We're camping out in the bonus room
upstairs, downing pints of frozen cream and watching all the
sappy movies possible. So, just the typical Saturday night at what
we've deemed the Spice House. Not because we can cook with a
wide variety of spices, but because of the range of attitudes under
one roof. At least that's Kenzie's explanation.

Kenzie stands up, gathering the garbage. "Maybe we should
switch to something salty. My tastebuds have lost their sensors
from the sugar overload."

"And I'm thinking we should watch something with a little
more action to it," I say. "We've predicted the last few movies with
weird accuracy."

Yes, we might've started our movie marathon at two this afternoon, but it's only eight now. The night is still young.

No, I'm not wallowing after the mishaps of the night before.
I'm consoling a friend after a rough week. At least that's what I'm
telling myself.

"Let's order in. Maybe some substantial protein and veggies

will help." Kenzie stands and raises her hands into the air, stretching.

I roll my eyes. "Really? You're going to worry about your diet now after at least three thousand calories of ice cream?"

Footsteps on the stairs cause me to turn and I see Evie, another roommate, walking up. She's got a couple of white bags in her hands. From the smell of it, she's bringing Chinese.

"I figured you all needed something to eat while you mope about your lack of boyfriends. I owe you both for the last time we ordered in. Here are your favorites."

Kenzie and I descend on the bags as though we haven't seen real food in days.

"Thanks, Evie. I'll send you money right now," I say, pulling out my phone.

"No, I told you I already owe you for last time. How about I get to pick the movie?" She reaches over and picks up the remote control. "I need a break from making jewelry."

I exchange a quick glance with Kenzie and we nod in agreement.

"Okay, but can it be in color this time?" Kenzie asks.

Evie is an old soul and her love of historical movies is fun for me. Kenzie isn't a fan though.

"I think we can manage that," she says. Evie scrolls through one of our streaming apps, the cost of which we all share.

More footsteps approach and another roommate, Millie appears.

"Whoa, you look like you got attacked by a bear," Kenzie says.

Millie's hair is matted at one side, and it looks like orange goo is in some sections on the other. A large brown stain along the front makes me hope it's just spilled chocolate. Although as a nanny to three small kids, I doubt that's the case.

"No bears, just toddlers." She tries to smile but falls onto the couch next to Evie.

"I take it the nannying is going well," I say, trying to add in the sarcasm. But Millie still hasn't caught on to my kind of humor.

She's the sweetest girl I've ever met, coming from a small town in the south. Boston is a big city and there are times when I wonder if she'll stick around through the end of her year-long contract.

She gives me a tiny smile, more like a grimace, and says, "It's going okay. It's hard when I'm with the kids all day and try to establish rules and then their parents come home and break every single one of them. So now they're all kinds of crazy because their mother doesn't think they should have a bedtime and loads them with sugar by the truckload."

I lean over and use my foot to slowly drag one of the ice cream tubs we'd forgotten to throw away out of Millie's view.

"Dani, I'm not against sugar," she says, letting out a small chuckle. "I'm just tired and want to blame my troubles on it at the moment. Do you have any left?"

Her comment causes an uproar of laughter throughout the room. In true Kenzie fashion, she walks over to where the few DVDs are stored and pulls out a giant-sized Hershey's chocolate bar.

"Whoa, Kenzie, you splurged for the chocolate with almonds kind, huh?" I tease.

"This was all they had left at the store when I went. I just throw away the almonds." Kenzie hands Millie the large bar and sinks into the cushion next to her.

My phone pings and I reach out to grab it from the coffee table.

A notification for the Love, Austen app is there.

You have 1 new match.

I'm still not exactly sure how it works. Rachelle's cousin, Tiffany, explained it all once, but I haven't seen her in a while because she's been on bedrest for her first pregnancy. I make a mental note to go see her.

There might be some questions as to why I'm on a match-making app when I keep striking out in my dating life. To be honest, I don't think dating apps work. But I'm a sucker for a chance to win anything, especially another trip, and signed up for the app while on the cruise with my brother, Landon.

Was luck on my side to win said trip? No, not at all.

I click through to the app, nearly forgetting the small party we've created. I'd had a fair amount of men messaging, but their line of conversation usually started out with a cheesy pickup line and then baseless conversation after.

Things had died down over the past few weeks because I got too busy to answer. At the time I'd been semi-dating Cameron, graduating, and trying to find a job. Not much time to spend messaging potential suitors.

The profile pops up of my messenger, a picture of a gorgeous sunset at the top of the page with several interests below. It never states the full name of the match, allowing anonymity until both parties agree to meet or continue the relationship.

Before I make it through several of the interests, a notification appears near the chat button.

Guy: Hi.

Well, this one is already doing better than the last fifteen. Some had been a match, while others had just gone through messaging anyone they thought might respond. I would rather become a hermit than date some of the guys I've managed to "meet" through here.

I stare at the screen for several moments until another message comes in. Does it show someone else that I'm active? Because I hate that. Where is the full anonymity in these matchmaker apps? I'm not good at ghosting people.

Guy: I just joined Love, Austen. It looks like we matched and I figured I'd message and get to know you a little better.

Points for getting to the heart of things. And at least he didn't say, "Hey hot stuff. Want to hook up later?"

Me: Welcome.

Not my most brilliant moment but I'm probably dealing with some guy sitting in his underwear in his parents' basement. How would I guess that? Experience, ladies. Not with apps, but with people in general.

Guy: What's your favorite thing to do?

Me: Read the profile, man. I didn't make it through that list of a billion questions for nothing.

I chuckle to myself, which draws Kenzie's attention.

"What are you smirking at over there? Are you going to accept or reject Evie's choice of a dog lover movie?"

With a quick glance, a picture of a boy and a dog are on the screen. "As much as I love dogs, I vote nay."

"Okay then, choice number two is Harry Potter."

The vote is unanimous and the girls settle in. I adjust in the small armchair and wait for a response as the little conversation bubble pops up in the message screen.

Guy: Touché. A woman who doesn't like to waste time. I like it.

Me: If that's supposed to be an innuendo, I'm out like trout.

Guy: No, no, no.

There's a pause, and I see the bubble pop up and disappear a few times before the message comes through.

Guy: Sorry, this is my first time on one of these things and I'm still new. I'll know better to think through every answer at least ten ways before pressing send from now on.

Me: You've learned well, Young Padawan.

Yes, I'm terrible, but like they say, talking online makes a person braver.

Guy: Okay, Star Trek reference. Good to know. Have you ever been to a Red Sox game?

I shake my head, laughing at the mix-up for the Star Wars reference.

Me: Do you mean have I ever lived since I've grown up in Boston? Yes, yes I have. I haven't sat as closely as I would like, but the outfield is still a great place to catch a ball.

Guy: Who's the one with the innuendo now?

And now I'm done. I tuck my phone away and try to focus on the fact that my roommates have turned on the movie with Dolores Umbridge in it. The lady drives me bonkers.

My phone buzzes against my backside and I pull it out, seeing several more messages from the mystery man.

Guy: Don't go. I'm sorry about that.

Guy: I don't usually talk like this.

Guy: Would you like to go out this weekend?

I frown, not sure what was wrong with the guy on the other end. At least I hope he's my age and not someone four decades older.

I'll have to ask Tiffany about that. Not that I plan on using this all the time.

Me: I'm not sure that would be a good idea. I'm not feeling a connection here.

I don't have to wait long for an answer.

Guy: I've totally felt one and we've been ma—

Seconds tick by and I'm watching the screen out of curiosity.

Guy: I sincerely apologize for the above conversations. My friend decided to take things into his own hands about my dating life.

I glance up at the TV, trying to figure out what to say to that. The tone on the last message was more formal than the others had been. It's a possibility it tells the truth, but I'm not sure about it.

Me: No problem. Good luck with all that.

I breathe out a sigh and turn off the notifications for the app in my settings. I didn't need to worry about some weirdo messaging me. That is the big sign my romantic life is going nowhere and fast.

CHAPTER 4
Miles

Nothing is worse than one of my best friends messaging someone without talking to me first.

I've gone through the messages a few more times and there's something about the woman's answers that intrigue me. She's direct and resolute, a lot like the woman I had dinner with the other night. Dani.

I still have her business card on my dresser. Even though I'm ticked at Jack for all he did the night before, there is some measure of reality there.

Do I want to keep avoiding my mother by dating women who walk through my life like a revolving door? Or could I get someone who sticks around a bit longer and helps me get past all the insecurity crap Tanya left in her wake?

Actually, a woman shouldn't have to do anything, but a support system helps.

I walk to my room and pick up the business card. Maybe Dani would be up for something like that. I mean, the people we were dating decided to make out with each other. We could be mutual partners in the fight against love. A small surge of triumph rises but fizzles quickly.

How did my life come to this?

Instead of making the call, I head down to the workout room in my apartment building and work up a sweat for a few hours.

The mental pro and con list to fake dating has been building ever since I completed the test the night before. And then, obviously not thinking clearly, I'd given Jack his phone without logging out of the system.

It wasn't until the end of the hockey game that I noticed him enthralled with something. Whoever had to endure his messages, I hope they find someone much better than what my account has provided.

After a shower and a large breakfast, I finally dial the number from Dani's business card. For some reason, my fingers are shaking, as if I'm fourteen again, getting ready to call a girl for the first time.

The phone rings a few times, heading to voicemail.

This is Dani. Leave a message and maybe I'll get back to you.

I smile at that, remembering our adventures at The Riptide. When the buzzer beeps, I hurry through, trying to figure out what to say. "Hey Dani, this is Miles Clark. I'm calling to see if we can get together." Is that too forward? I mean, we had an amazing conversation about books and places to travel. My mouth makes the decision for me by saying, "To, um, discuss the dry-cleaning bill."

I wince and hang up, knowing that's probably the worst idea I've ever had, but she was so determined to pay me back, maybe this will get her to meet me.

"And then what, Miles?" I say to myself in the mirror. "Dry cleaning is the bait and hook method? First of all, you're lying to get her there and then you're going to ask her to be your fake girlfriend?"

A message pops up from my mother. A reminder to not be late for lunch with some potential clients.

I pull out a suit from my walk-in closet, choosing a tie that's brighter than normal. Maybe it will help get rid of some of the irritation flooding through me.

Because lunch with Mom is more of an interrogation than a normal conversation. And if Dani says no, I'll have to go with whoever is on the other end of the matchmaker app.

My options for a fake relationship are limited.

CHAPTER 5
Dani

T he moment I see my boss's name pop up on my phone, I know something is wrong.

"Danielle, I thought I was clear you wouldn't use that particular company for the catering." Not the best call to wake up to on a Sunday morning.

I'm still in pjs but I pull every notebook I own onto the bed surrounding me and my laptop in front of me.

"Please, it's Dani. And it's not the same company, Sharon," I say, doing everything I can to keep my tone light and fluffy. I've already had an incident with her this week and I don't need her to think I'm being stubborn. "I wrote down here that I shouldn't use That's a Toast Catering and the company I've contracted for the mixer is Taste & Fun Catering." Both names are lame, but I know they are different because I've checked. And the notes I have from talking with Sharon are triple underlined. I didn't forget.

Silence takes over and only the sound of her heavy breathing echoes through the phone.

"Okay, I'm going over the guest list. We're going to need a better draw, Danielle. We need a multi-millionaire or someone who can help us attract more alumni to these kinds of things."

I pause a moment, shaking off her use of my first name. Her

words sink in. "I thought this function was to give other alumni a chance to connect." I had pictured a casual evening with people chatting about their businesses, not a New York fashion show with money falling from the sky. Not that I'd ever seen that.

"Correct. But the ones you've got on the list already are lower-level. We need someone who can make a splash." Papers shuffle and she says, "I'll send you a list of potential alumni you'll need to start calling. We need this function to go well so they'll start donating to the university."

Ahh, there it is. The real reason she's putting so much pressure on me for this. Half of me wants to just hang up the phone and let her deal with it. I hate being micromanaged and that's pretty much what's been happening since I started a couple weeks ago. Let me do my job, and if I fail, I'll own up to it.

"Will do. Send me the list and I'll get started." Once I end the call, I let out a soft cry, knowing I can't full out scream my frustrations or I'll wake up the rest of the house.

I pack up one of my notebooks and my laptop, opting to continue working out on the back porch. At least I can pretend my Sunday morning will be full of adventure if I'm not staring at four walls.

I've got two weeks until the mixer, and I've got to get on top of the details before Sharon runs away with them.

"You look like you've been run over by a train," Millie says from the kitchen table as I make my way through the kitchen.

"I feel it. You don't have to work today?"

Millie shakes her head. "No, the kids are in Maine with their grandparents. Now I just need to figure out what to do."

"You could always go on a walking tour of Boston. Or you could be amazing and help me call wealthy men. And women." There's got to be women on the list. Sharon better not be discriminating based on gender. I take in a deep breath, hoping it will soothe my irritation.

"I think I'll pass on that, thanks," Millie says, taking another bite of cereal.

"Your loss. I mean, who doesn't want to have people hang up on them all day today?" My laugh is almost a plea for help.

I head out to the swing and set up, my phone charged and ready for several phone calls.

Sharon's email is stuck in the Spam folder and the email below it catches my eye. It's from Love, Austen.

Curiosity kills me and I click on it, wondering if they've sent official results of my matches or whatnot. Maybe if I find someone I'm actually matched with, instead of the guys claiming we've been matched, that would be a step in the right direction.

Guy: Again, I apologize for last night.

It's always so different to read tone into words on a screen, but everything about the message makes me think it might be another guy.

But maybe that's the draw. He seems like a punk, strikes out, and then pretends to be someone completely different when his ship is sinking.

I hover the cursor over the button to delete and decide against it at the moment. Instead, I highlight the email from Sharon and the message from Love, Austen and drag them to my inbox.

But I don't have time to dwell on the message, so I open the spreadsheet, grateful someone had thought to include phone numbers. That will make it a lot easier to get the calls in.

After ten minutes, I've called fifteen people and only spoken to two, the rest heading to voicemail. The beauty of the cold call.

I'm onto the C's now and a quick scroll through the rest of the document tells me this will be a few days' worth of calls. Why did I want the job I have again? Because the idea of putting together parties and getting paid for it while helping build a college booster club sounded perfect for a communications major.

I move my finger to the screen, reading Miles Clark and then drag it over to the phone number. Dialing, I hope I get a response.

"Hey, I'm glad you called back so soon," a deep voice says on the other end.

I pull my phone away from my ear to check the number. It's

not one I recognize and with all that's been happening lately, my brain remembers nothing.

With the phone back next to my ear, I say, "Sorry? This is Dani Higgins with Boston University. I'm calling about—"

"So you got my message then? Are you free to meet this afternoon?"

For the second time within moments, I'm speechless. "I'm sorry, I haven't received any messages. I'm calling from the Development Office at Boston University. We are holding a mixer in two weeks—"

"Sorry to interrupt, Dani. This is Miles. We met at The Riptide."

And right there, my stomach drops out and I'm frozen. Like Anna frozen. But unlike her, true love is not going to help me out of this situation.

Or maybe it could. I'm not sure of much anymore.

"Hey Miles. Sorry, I've been working most of the morning. You said you left a message?" And on cue, the small voicemail icon appears at the top of my screen.

"Yeah, I thought we could get together and talk about something."

I glance back at the screen. Cold calling people on the list isn't helping. Maybe meeting in person would.

"Sure," I say, "I'm free this afternoon or evening or most afternoons next week." Ugh. That sounded way too available, desperate even. I don't need him thinking I'm trying to wiggle my way into being his girlfriend. The guy is hot, but even a daydream of it is laughable. In twenty years, we'd tell our kids I'd thrown a large soda all over him the first time we met. Not going to happen.

And then the brakes go full force in my brain. Marriage isn't in the cards for me. Guys just hang out with me until someone better comes along.

"This afternoon works. Where should we meet?" His voice is deep and reminds me of melted chocolate.

"Uh, how about Boston Common?" There is a T-stop there

and then I won't have to walk far. Not like I'm overdoing it this morning anyway.

"Done. How about four?" Miles's voice sounds like there is hope brimming there. Is he hoping I'll pay for his dry cleaning? That's definitely what this is. I'll have to transfer some money from my bank to my credit card to afford it.

I nod and say, "Sounds good."

After a long breath, I pull my computer closer to me. I might as well look him up so I can figure out how to convince him to come to the mixer. Maybe he's one of the lower-level alumni Sharon mentioned.

After a few clicks, there's at least twenty-seven million hits according to the webpage. Miles has his own Wikipedia page. How is that possible?

I click on a more reputable link, claiming Miles was at an event to support the local Children's Hospital, but that's the only line about him in the entire article. I need details.

Wikipedia it is.

Miles Clark, 28. Heir to the Clark Medical Group empire.

Okay, I vaguely remember Amber saying something about that.

A link just a bit lower shows him as one of the youngest in the industry, and another says he's one of the wealthiest men in town.

Great. This guy is like Boston royalty. What is a little more humiliation, right?

Anger burns through me. The guy wants me to foot the bill for his suit and he probably makes my yearly salary in a week.

I sigh, remembering that I'm the one who offered to pay for it.

And meeting him in person will hopefully help me know what to say to get him to the mixer. Because I doubt there's anyone higher on the alumni success list than Miles Clark.

CHAPTER 6
Miles

I'm pacing back and forth in the Common. There are so many thoughts running through my brain, and I've almost left at least five times.

When did my life resort to fake dating?

My mind brings up a photo of my mother. I know she means well, but she attacks my relationships like she does anything else in her life, personal or business—like a bulldog. As though tomorrow will end and the chance will have passed.

It makes me miss Dad even more. He was good for Anita Clark, helping her navigate society with a little more tact.

Now that's my job and I'm failing at it.

My mom and dad met at a dog park of all places. She was out for a walk with her German Shepherd and he was walking his neighbor's dog. Serendipity at its finest.

But I'm not sure that would be the key to finding a woman worth marrying anymore. My parents didn't have wealth to impede them at the time.

Even after major business deals and all the other high-intensity events I've been through, I'm sweating more at what I'm about to do.

A fake relationship. I never thought I'd have to do that kind of thing.

But when the woman I thought I was going to marry told me she's done and to stop calling, it kind of broke me. And I'm not ready for any pushing my mother does for me to settle down with a woman of her choosing.

So, this is the right course. And if Dani says no, I'll message the gal Jack talked to the night before.

"Hey Miles," Dani says, casually walking up to me.

"Dani, thanks for coming." Her eyes widen, worry etched on her face. I realize all my attempts at being cryptic are more sketchy than the shoes I've seen a few people wearing around this afternoon. I wave to a bench. "Do you want to sit?"

She frowns. "I got your message. This is just about dry cleaning, right? Or do I need to pay for a new suit? Again, I apologize about Sodagate. Just tell me the number and I'll pay it." With her eyes closed, she sucks in a deep breath, looking as though she's ready to go diving in the Charles River.

I open my mouth and pause a few seconds. "Actually, no. My suit will be fine. And I wouldn't make you pay for it even if it was ruined."

She opens her eyes, and I note they're a pale blue beneath her glasses, standing out against her slightly tanned skin.

Confused, she says, "Okay, did I leave something at dinner the other night?"

I blow out a breath and say, "I didn't think you'd come if I texted what I hope you'll consider."

She scoots as far against the bench armrest as possible, several inches from me. "And this is why we meet in a public park," she mumbles to herself.

I can't help but laugh. "I'm sorry, my life is weird and complicated, and I hoped you would help me out with a few things."

"You want me to help you with a few things? Isn't that what assistants are for?" She blinks at me, her pursed lips drawing my gaze. What would it be like to kiss them?

Where did that come from? I haven't felt even a spark of attraction in months with any of the women I've dated and here I am jumping into thoughts of kissing?

Running a hand along the back of my neck, I should've run through this before coming here.

"I need someone to be my fake girlfriend for a few weeks." There, I said it. The words are out and now to see the aftermath.

Her mouth is half-open, and she looks stunned. "Fake date. And you're asking me? Am I on a reality tv show? Did Ashton Kutcher get back into the game?" She's searching the park and I'm losing steam.

"Why are you surprised I'd ask you?"

She holds up one finger. "Because we met when our dates were making out and I doused you in Dr Pepper." Finger two goes up. "Your other date is a lot more refined than I'll ever be." She shivers before holding up three fingers. "And I'm not into dating at the moment. This girl does not need any more heartbreaks."

There's a vulnerability in her eyes that disappears within seconds.

I pause, giving her some time to process what she just said. "Okay, listen. My mother is a great woman, but when it comes to marrying off her only son, she starts to act like this is the ultimate trophy she's never won. Ever since my ex-girlfriend and I broke up, she spent months trying to get us to 'accidentally meet up' which didn't work out well. Especially because she keeps trying to fly me to New York for non-existent business meetings."

Dani grimaces. "That's not awkward at all."

"I've gone out with at least fifteen women she's approved of and a few she hasn't. But my bachelor status going into event season is going to make things difficult and I don't need her pushing another woman at me."

"What is event season? Is that like wedding season without the pretty dress?" Dani's face is curious but the dry humor in it causes me to laugh.

"Event season is basically the Clarks parading around to all the charity auctions and the social gatherings of Boston. It's long and dreadful, but I'd rather do it with someone who has no interest in me whatsoever."

"Are you trying to rile your mom up? Like, you're hoping to drive her crazy at this point?" There's a ghost of a smile on her lips and my hopes rise.

I pause, thinking that over. "Not really crazy, just enough to leave me alone."

"So, in summary, you're saying Mother Goose is ready to get you married off and you're not quite ready for that commitment yet?" Dani asks.

"Um, I'm sorry. Did you just say Mother Goose? As in the nursery rhymes?" I'm having a hard time keeping it together after that.

Dani laughs, and a small amount of relief passes through me. "Yeah, it was the only thing I could think of at the moment."

I should probably stop teasing, but I love the sound of her laugh and I don't want her to stop. "So, not Eros?"

She gives me a strange look and says, "I'm surprised you know who that is."

I tone my smile down a bit, curious as to what she means. "That Eros is the Greek god of love?" When she nods, I say, "Okay, so what's your first impression of me?"

"What if we walk and talk about this? I need sustenance and some time to gather my thoughts about your sudden proposal. Er —I mean, request." Dani stands and walks in the direction of the graveyard next to the Common.

As we walk by, I point and say, "These people are dead. I doubt they need much in the way of vitamins and minerals at this point."

"True, but one of my favorite places is just a short walk from here." She leads me to Faneuil Hall, where there are several food options inside, almost like a restaurant market. She orders a chocolate strawberry crepe and I get the same before handing over my card to pay quickly, knowing she'll be bugged.

"You don't have to do that, you know," she says, her eyes raised as if I should be scared.

"I want to. I'm the one who invited you out on this excursion."

She nods and takes a bite of the crepe before we've even walked down to the small section of tables. "So delicious. Someday I'll go to France and eat my weight in crepes."

My laughter pulls her out of her trance, and I almost feel bad. After taking a bite of my own crepe, I have to say it's not bad. Although French ones are definitely better.

"Are you making fun of my future plans, sir?" It's difficult to hold back a laugh at her attempt of a French accent.

I shake my head. "Not making fun of it, just enjoying the fact that you are passionate about things."

"Food. I'm passionate about food, Miles." She pauses a moment and a slow smile appears.

I raise my hands in surrender. "I didn't say it was bad."

She takes another bite of the crepe, her eyes watching my face without blinking. I wish I knew what she was thinking behind those striking blue eyes.

"Okay, back to your impression of me." I lean forward, ducking down a bit to catch her eye.

She pats her mouth with a napkin and glances up. I'm able to take in more of her features and while I hadn't noticed the night at The Riptide, she's quite beautiful. Hopefully she has no mind reading capabilities.

"Originally, I figured you were a stiff businessman who is tough enough to not even care about his date making out with someone else."

I nod. "It's because I ate the food, huh?"

She stretches one hand toward me, most likely for emphasis. "You ate the food. It's like the ultimate burn for a relationship. I was in awe."

"In awe? Or just hungry?"

With a nod, she says, "Probably a little of that too. It made me rethink the Big Breakup."

I raise my eyebrows, surprised by her answer. "What's the Big Breakup?"

She takes another bite of her crepe and glances around, watching a couple pass us. I'm wondering if she'll ever get to the point when she looks back at me.

"I had just come back from Christmas break. Clay, my ex-boyfriend, and I had been dating for over five years and I might have...well, my sisters convinced me that he would probably pop the question."

"Oh," is all I say. I can see where this is going and wish I could help in anyway. Except she's single and talking about the past.

"We're at dinner in the North End, a fun little pasta place, and I'm all hyped with the idea that I might be getting engaged and that I'll be able to plan my wedding throughout the last months of college," she says, waving her hands several times. "And then he says, 'Danielle, I want to break up.' I keep it together long enough to empty my plate of spaghetti on top of his head and then leave."

Not the twist I'd been expecting. Then again, Dani is a lot stronger than I expect.

"That sounds like an adequate response."

She shakes her head. "Not now. I'm thinking I should've sat there and tortured him with my presence a bit longer. Made him pay for the meal and then headed out of there."

I grin. "Personally, I wish I'd been there for the spaghetti dumping."

A few seconds pass as we both finish our crepes and head outside into the warm summer air. More like humid.

"I'm not sure it was a slip but you just called yourself Danielle. Is there a reason you're so against the use of your full name?"

Dani blows out a breath and frowns. "Everyone else in my life calls me Dani, except my ex. He'd called me Danielle from the very beginning and I thought it was sweet, endearing even. Now it just makes me want to throw up as it reminds me of him."

I nod, understanding more than I thought I would. "I have similar problems. Not with my name, but random things that make me mad when I see them, all because of my ex-girlfriend."

We walk several steps, heading closer to the harbor.

"So, back to your original proposal," Dani says before her cheeks go a lovely rosy color. "I mean, uh, your business proposal. How long are you thinking? A couple weeks?"

I rub my chin, feeling the whiskers there even after the clean shave hours ago. "I hadn't thought that far just yet. Would you be up for at least until the middle of August? That's when most of the parties and events slow down. Well, until they pick up again in the fall."

"That's like what? Ten weeks?" She nods and says, "Yeah. I'm game. We'll have to establish a few rules first, but this could be fun."

"Rules like what?"

She blinks a few times and says, "I don't know. My only frame of reference for a fake relationship is that teen movie about the girl whose love letters get sent to all her old crushes. There were definitely rules in that one."

I shrug. "I've never heard of it, but yeah, sounds good."

She squints her eyes a bit as she faces me fully. "Can I ask one tiny little favor?"

And all the great feelings I'd had spending the afternoon with her on a not-real date blow out like a storm on a windy day. This is what always happens. I get close and then they start requesting favors. Money. Gifts. Then again, she is agreeing to help me out.

"Sure. What do you need?" I say, trying to keep my voice light.

"The reason I originally called you today was that you're on the list of 'acceptable' candidates to invite to our mixer at BU in a couple weeks. Will you come?"

I pause, surprised. "Of all the things you could've asked for and that's it?"

Her lips part, like she wants to say something but isn't completely sure what just yet.

"So, that's a no?" she asks, her lips turning down.

"No, that's a yes. You're helping me out. The least I can do is make your job a little easier."

She blows out a long breath and gives a quick squeal. "Thank you, so much. You don't know how much that means. My boss has been on me to find more people to draw in so it will eventually benefit the university, which I think is lame. But I guess funding and all that is kind of important in a career like mine."

I chuckle as she babbles on. "It would be my honor to escort you to my alumni mixer."

Dani laughs. "Okay, Sir Miles of the Round Table. It's a deal."

"As for the rules," she begins, and I have to laugh.

I nod. "Okay, let's go over those. We'll probably want to keep it low key, not telling anyone about it. I don't need my mother thinking I've lost my mind."

"Well, you just did propose to fake date. That either means you're crazy or your mother is way too involved."

"True," I say, laughing. "What else do you think needs to be on our list?"

"PDA. Public display of affection. Only when necessary." Dani is bent over her phone taking notes on an app.

I try not to smile when I say, "So, no kissing at the doorstep when I drop you off?"

Her head snaps up and her cheeks go a dark shade of red before she nods. "Yes, that's probably not a good idea. We have to sell this relationship, but extra kissing makes things confusing." Her gaze is distant, and I want to know what she's thinking. Maybe her lost opportunities with her ex-boyfriend?

Instead, I say, "Yeah, that works. We'll hug at appropriate times." I swallow hard and turn away from her face when I say, "And kiss if necessary, but in public."

Again, why am I pushing the kissing?

Her laughter is like the sound of a bomb going off and I

jump, surprised by how loud it is. "Yes, kissing only when necessary."

"I can't imagine too many people thinking we need to kiss."

"Then you don't know my family," Dani says. I don't know why but she looks a little disappointed. Is it from my comment or hers?

"I'm sure that would be an adventure. Anything else?"

She shrugs, glancing over the notes on her phone again. "Let me think about it some more. I mean, you just sprung this on me."

"True," I say, swallowing hard. I'm so relieved she's actually said yes that I'm rushing things.

"We'll end things on August fifteenth." She finishes typing and glances up. "Are we going to need to do a public breakup? Or is this one of those things you send a statement into the media that says, 'Please give us the space we need at this time'?"

Her face is so serious that I can't help but laugh. "I'm sure we can do whatever you want to do."

"This is your arena. I'm just the guest of honor." Dani smiles and I relax a bit.

"How about we figure that out when we get to it?"

She sticks out her hand to seal the deal, and all I can think about is that this fake thing might not be too hard. But then again, there's the danger of falling for her. The woman is drawing me in like an oasis in the desert.

I just hope this time won't be as hard as my last relationship when things turn out to be a mirage.

CHAPTER 7
Dani

I went to the meeting with Miles thinking I'd have to do some hard-hitting negotiation just to get the guy to agree to my weird plan. Instead, he comes at me with something I'll rate an eleven on the strange scale.

The idea of Dani Higgins going to high society events as a girlfriend of one of the wealthiest bachelors in Boston is laughable. I can dress up for a night out with the girls, and I'm an expert at the comfy attire known as yoga pants and a t-shirt. But I'd probably have to wear some formal gowns to these things. I didn't even get to do that more than once in high school.

Add that to the list of things I regret about my past relationship with Clay. The guy couldn't understand why I would want to go to school dances when we were already dating. "Those are for the people who don't have a boyfriend or girlfriend." Then he'd turn around and go back to his video game.

Gosh, what did I even see in him?

I guess that's what can happen with a first love.

Once I get home from one of the strangest yet fun afternoons I've had in a while, I find Kenzie holed up in her room, and I can't help but relay the whole story. Having her on my side will help keep my sanity throughout this adventure.

"You're going to fake date him?" she asks with disbelief in her expression. So maybe I overestimated her willingness to help me out.

It's not until then that I realize I've broken the first rule. Crap, this is going to be harder than I thought.

"Yeah, I mean, I'll probably get eaten alive at some of these events, but at least we'll both get what we need, right? Just make sure you don't tell anyone, pretty please?" But her question makes me wonder if this is going to be worth it just for him to come to my event.

She puts her forefinger and thumb together next to the side of her lips and pulls them across, as if zipping them together.

"Is it a bad idea?" I say, not realizing my words aren't just in my head.

"It's a fake relationship," Kenzie says. "I've never heard of anyone in real life needing something like this. But in all the movies the couples usually end up together."

I laugh, tipping my head back at the thought of Miles ever falling in love with me. I mean, my track record isn't really helping that fantasy either.

Kenzie pulls out her laptop and starts tapping away. I slide up next to her on the bed, leaning over to see what she's looking up.

Miles Clark girlfriend.

The webpage is flooded with pictures of Miles and the woman next to him, who's pretty much the opposite of me. She's got rich dark curls and makes every dress she wears look like it was made for her.

"Yeah," I say, forcing a laugh. "Love isn't on the docket when you compare me to her."

"What are you talking about?" Kenzie says. "You're gorgeous. And you don't even wear makeup. Not fair."

"Yeah, tell that to the line of guys waiting out the door for me." This time my sarcasm hits my chest.

"Just because you've dated crappy guys doesn't mean you

don't have a chance of being with a guy like Miles." Kenzie's eyes light up.

"Weren't you the one a few minutes ago who didn't believe this whole thing?" Kenzie tries to speak but I put up a finger. "How about we focus on what I'm supposed to do instead of trying to convince me I'm compatible with the guy." A small voice in my head worries that I might fall for him. With the afternoon we'd had, casual and fun, it's a possibility on my end. That's all I need: to be rejected by a billionaire.

My phone rings and I smile as I glance down at the number. Miles The Boyfriend. It's probably better not to leave visual clues around that we're fake dating, so this was the best I could get without letting my poor brain think this is real.

"Hey!"

"Hey Dani. I wanted to call and thank you for a fun afternoon. And to ask if you have time to go shopping this week? We forgot to hammer out those details."

"Shopping? Like for clothes?"

Kenzie's hands are up to her mouth in no-time to keep from screaming out and I'm grateful so Miles doesn't hear.

"Yes, for clothes," he says. "I figure if you're doing this for me, you might as well be comfortable."

My eyes focus on the computer screen, the fancy dresses the woman is wearing at events next to Miles.

"Yeah, so comfy." How do they even keep all the body parts from popping out of those kinds of outfits?

"I'll have Sonia, my personal shopper, help us out."

Instead of continuing to repeat his words, I mouth them to Kenzie, who starts bouncing up and down on the bed, clapping her hands together.

"Okay, yeah, whatever you think is best." Because honestly, I'm on par with Amelia from The Princess Diaries, pre-makeover. I'll take any help I can get.

"Great, I have a light day on Tuesday. Will that work?"

I nod, forgetting that he can't see me. "Um, yeah. That sounds great. I can work through lunch and be off around four."

"Sounds good. I'll pick you up then."

No sooner do I push end when Kenzie yells and screams in excitement. I just sink back onto the bed and stare at the ceiling. Maybe this whole thing is scripted by Ashton Kutcher for his Punk'd show. But I hope to end up on the good side of that one if it is.

CHAPTER 8

Dani

Why did I train myself that it's okay to be a procrastinator? It's the morning of our shopping excursion and I'm trying to decide on an outfit that will be considered business casual and also work for an afternoon of shopping. With a personal shopper.

I still can't believe Miles has one of those. And if I had some shred of fashion sense, it could be a fun career.

My boss had been excited for a few minutes that I'd convinced Miles Clark to come, but then got mad that I hadn't found another ten like him. Again, adulting is hard.

"Are you all right?" Evie asks, peeking around my closet door.

"I don't know," I whine, sitting down on my bed. It's covered in all the other outfits I've tried on but haven't organized back into place just yet. I usually border on clean freak, but my brain can't handle that right now.

Evie's gaze scans the room. "Is there something happening at work?"

"No," I say slowly. I've managed to keep a secret from my other two roommates, but that's only since we all work at strange hours during the week. "It's one of those days where nothing fits or I don't like it."

I stand and walk to the closet, hoping by some magic that I'll have at least one shirt worthy of my afternoon. A floral blouse is hanging from the rod, and it makes me feel like I should be eating dinner at 4 pm and falling asleep in the recliner any time I sit down, but it's so comfortable that I keep it around. Then there's a new blouse I bought several months ago for what I thought would be an engagement date.

I pull it out, a teal flowy top and walk to where Evie can see it. She's so good, just over there folding a few of my neglected pants choices.

"What do you think?" I ask, holding it up in front of me.

Evie smiles. "That color looks great on you. Go for it."

I nod, walking back into the small closet and taking off another shirt I didn't like.

"So, um, is there someone's eye you're hoping to catch?" Evie calls.

My laugh comes out more like a snort. "Not at the moment. I just hoped I'd be able to avoid the wrath of my boss by not looking like a schlub."

My phone rings on the bed, and I lunge to grab it before she sees Miles and his title. I should've changed it to FB instead of The Boyfriend. I don't know why I get pleasure from saying or thinking that.

"Why does your phone say Miles The Boyfriend?" Evie's eyes narrow in on mine. "Are you dating again?"

I press my lips together, knowing I need to keep the secret. That question is going to be hitting me right and left in the coming weeks and I can't act like I've been given truth serum every time.

"It's kind of a new thing. I put that in there mostly as a joke," I say, pointing to my phone. Meanwhile the call ends and a few seconds later, he calls again.

"A joke? Do you work with him or something?" Evie's eyes soften.

I blow out a breath. "Kind of. It's recent, though."

Evie takes a step forward, placing her hand on my left shoulder and says, "If you're ready to jump into the dating pool, I'm here for you. If not, I get it."

My smile feels a whole lot shakier than it should, and while I haven't exactly lied, the guilt seeps in. Evie has been through a lot in her life, or so I've heard from small snippets Kenzie has relayed to me, and here she is, telling me that she'll be by my side no matter what.

At least I know I'll have people there to pick up the pieces once this thing is all over.

"Thanks, girl. We'll see how it goes."

Evie leaves with a confused expression and I pick up the third time Miles calls, hoping it's not an emergency or anything. Then again, we don't know each other well enough to know what constitutes an emergency.

"Hi, change of plan if you're up for it." Miles's voice sounds so far away. What does a change mean for him?

I nod, even though he can't see me. "Sure, I'm good with whatever. Do you need to go another time?"

"Tonight still works, but we'll get dinner first. I need to meet with an old investor of the company. He's here from Europe and this might be a good time to test our relationship."

I nearly drop the phone at his words because even though I know it's fake, the word relationship gets me every time.

I put the phone back up to my ear, my hands trembling. "Does that mean we can do a crash course on each other's lives?" My insides are screaming that I'm not ready for something like this. I thought we'd have time, a lot of time, to allow me to memorize all the facts I need to know about him. And now I'm down to minutes.

Miles chuckles. "For sure. I doubt there will be a lot of interrogation about our relationship at this dinner."

"So…" I let the word drag out a bit, wondering how to say this to a man whose wardrobe probably costs my salary for the year. "What should I wear to this?"

"Don't worry about that. I've got something for you to wear."

I nearly choke on that idea. A guy bringing me clothing I could wear to a dinner. Unheard of.

"You do realize I'm not a stick figure, right? Like, things don't always fit when I go to the store." A wave of embarrassment courses through me. Why did I call attention to my curves? Now he'll take note of them.

Without hesitation, Miles says, "It's fine. Sonia knows what she's doing."

I pause, trying to place the name again. Right, the personal shopper.

"Okay, I'll see you this afternoon then."

"I'm outside your house. At least I think I am." That's when my foot catches onto the silky material of a shirt and all my momentum takes me backward. I don't even have time to try and catch myself before I'm on the ground seeing stars.

"Are you okay?" I hear from my phone lying next to me.

I grab for it and manage to ask, "Bright yellow door?" I might as well test to see if he is outside.

"Uh-huh. And a whole bunch of flamingos in the front lawn."

I'd forgotten about those. They'd been a prank between Evie and our next-door neighbor. She'd accidentally started a prank war a few weeks ago and it's funny to see how it's escalated. Especially with how much she mothers us, seeing her let go a bit has been amazing.

"That would be us. I'll come meet you at the door."

I run downstairs, still in casual pants and my hair just barely dry.

"Where are you heading so fast?" Kenzie asks, glancing up from the computer in the front room of the house.

"To see a guy about an outfit." I don't stick around to see her face.

I'm on the porch as Miles gets out of his sleek black car. He looks just as good as the machine.

And that's when I have to do a mental block of all feelings related to Miles. There would never be an "us," so I don't allow myself even a sliver of hope there.

He's carrying a black bag. Ten bucks whatever's inside there is the wrong size.

When he sees me, he smiles. That's better than what Clay had done at the end of our relationship. I'd been an obligation, until Amber destroyed that. And for a moment, I wonder what she'll think of me dating Miles. Fake dating, but she won't have to know that.

"Looks like you're ready to go," he says, pointing to my taco-loving pants.

I smile drily. "Yeah, if we want to go to a Mexican restaurant, I'm all in. Tacos for life."

"As much as I'd like that, we're eating at Top Shelf tonight."

It takes a few moments for me to realize that my mouth is hanging open. Top Shelf is one of those restaurants you hear people going to, but you never have a hope that you'll be there. It's owned by one of the Boston Breeze hockey players but since I didn't know any famous athletes or people like Miles before this past week, I've never been.

And now I'm terrified about how I'm supposed to look. I take the bag, surprised that the brush of our fingers could create so much electricity buzzing through me. It's probably static electricity or something from his car. Right?

My mind is a fuzzy mess and I take a step back, trying to regain my balance.

"What time do you have to be to work?" Miles asks.

I glance down at my watch and see I've got a total of five minutes to get dressed and head out before I miss my bus. "In thirty-five minutes." I groan. So much for looking cute.

"Why don't you get ready and I can drop you off on my way to the office?"

I might have to reboot my brain because everything is coming in slow and fuzzy. A guy willing to move his schedule a bit to accommodate me? "You want to give me a ride to work?"

He shrugs. "Yeah, I mean, you seemed distressed about being late and I have to drive by there anyway."

"Thank you. I don't need any more glares from Sharon's office. Come in while I finish up." I open the door and walk in, waiting for him to enter before I close it.

"This is where you live, huh?" he says, his hands tucked into the pockets of a blue suit that is doing wonders for his figure. And that's when I have to relax and not worry about him or how good he looks. This is all pretend, make-believe. Maybe we need to cue up a few episodes of Mr. Roger's Neighborhood as a reminder of how that's supposed to go.

There is a small scuffle and I turn to see Evie with eyes wide as she takes him in. "Dani, you've brought a friend over." Her words are said through clenched teeth.

"Evie, this is Miles Clark. Miles, this is one of my roommates, Evie Evans."

With a more pointed look, Evie frowns and glances in my direction with her eyes wide. It's all starting to click. "Miles, huh?"

I'd purposely left off the title of why this man was here, looking like a GQ model in our humble abode. "Will you be okay here while I hurry and change?"

Miles looks down at a nice watch and says, "I can do that." He glances up at me with a grin and now I get the whole swoon part of romance movies. Thank goodness for this sturdy handrail because it's keeping me upright.

I force a smile and nod. "I'll hurry." A mental plan swirls in my head as I run up to my room. I'll just have to do my makeup in the car. Not a big deal.

It isn't until I get to my room and hear Kenzie's voice downstairs that I worry about what's going to happen next. She'll either scare him away or make things so awkward that I'll be wishing I'd just turned him down.

I didn't offer him a drink or a place to sit at all. Great first impression, Dani.

My fingers fumble with the zipper on the black bag and even though I'm trying to hurry in order to spare Miles from what I know will be a full interrogation by two of my roommates, it's taking longer because of the rush.

I finally get the zipper down and open the bag to see a beautiful burgundy blouse and a nice pair of black slacks. The feel of them is almost like my yoga pants and I'm wondering what other tips I can learn from this guy about fashion and comfort. All the business attire I've ever tried on were uncomfortable or itchy, but pulling on this outfit is like curling up with the softest blanket in the world. And it all fits. What kind of magic is this?

Maybe this is the cousin pair to the jeans the friends wore in *The Sisterhood of the Traveling Pants*.

I glance in the mirror, admiring the fit and the look. When my hair is done, I might pass for someone not just walking out of a business office. I'd have to figure out where he got these pants and buy them in all the colors to wear to work.

Now I sound like my mother.

I run a curling iron through my long hair, doing my best to keep it simple so I can hurry. The amount of laughter floating up from downstairs is making me anxious. I don't experience the fear of missing out too often, but this is definitely an exception.

Grabbing my phone and makeup bag, I head back down, not prepared for what looks like girls around a campfire listening to scary stories. Instead, it's three of my roommates on random chairs they've pulled up to listen to Miles, who's on the chair next to the computer desk.

"And then she turns, and Dr Pepper is flying through the air. Everything happened in slow motion."

"Great, are we retelling the DP events of the other night?" I say, embarrassment cropping up.

Millie turns and grins. "Of course. We needed the other side of the story."

"How did you get my side of the story?" I say, jabbing my pointer finger into my chest. Ow, that kind of hurt.

Evie and Millie turn to Kenzie.

She gives me a weak smile. "I might've let it slip." Now I just hope she can keep my secret without spilling the beans.

"Oh Dani, you look gorgeous," Evie says, standing and bridging the gap between us. She takes my hands and holds them out, looking at the shirt and outfit. "What are you doing wearing those though?" She points and I glance down at the casual flats I'd put on.

"They're black and they're comfortable."

Miles stands, and inside I'm panicking. Nothing like having my shoes scrutinized in front of my date. Fake date, I mean.

Evie takes my arm and spins around to Miles. "Give us just another minute."

He nods, looking like he's trying to hold back a smile. And all the emotions wash through me. No wonder no guy has ever stuck around with me. I'm not eye candy and my fashion sense is below the threshold.

"What's wrong, Dani?" Evie asks as she shuts the door to her room.

"I'm a social disgrace." The emotions are close to the surface, not in the I'm-going-to-cry-now kind of way, but in an I-shouldn't-have-agree-to-this sensation.

Evie settles her hands on my shoulders and waits until I look her in the eyes. "The guy out there doesn't think so."

I think of Miles. He's a lot different than most of the guys on his social level have ever been toward me. I wonder why there's a difference. From how it sounds, his mother isn't the most likeable person in the world.

"It's not like he's here for—" I break off, knowing I have to keep this to myself.

"What is he here for? I mean, you're an amazing person. Loyal, funny, adventurous. We typically don't have gentleman callers this early in the morning."

"Gentleman callers," I say with a laugh, sitting down on Evie's perfectly made bed.

"I know, I need to catch up with the times or whatever. It just seems like the early nineteen hundreds were simpler when it came to dating." Evie walks to her closet and disappears inside for a moment. Our house is small, but it has a lot of great quirks, like mini-walk-in closets. She comes out a few seconds later and hands me a pair of black open-toed high heels. "They didn't have to worry about dating apps or social media messing things up back in the good ole days. Wear these."

I give her a dry look. "Evie, have you ever seen me wear high heels? They're like death traps waiting for a good hole in the ground to help me go flying. I'm not a bird."

Evie laughs and shakes her head. "Well, for the time being, you've got an attractive guy who you can cling to if something like that happens."

She has a point. Which makes me think of touching Miles. Under that suit, he's probably got an amazing body. As the heat rushes through my chest, I shake off those thoughts and remember that I'm trying to be punctual to work. At least we set up the ground rules early.

I slip on the shoes and stand up. "I feel like I should be at the circus right now."

"No circus. Just an awesome restaurant with a hot, rich guy." Evie wags her eyebrows at me.

"In eight hours," I groan, not too excited about having to go to work in between. I just want to do my job and make it awesome, but there's always the constant worry of Sharon looking over my shoulder as I work.

I roll my eyes and we head toward the door. Evie stops and says, "I think I have a clutch that will match your outfit as well."

She's back in seconds with a small, shiny black clutch. I grin at her. "You don't think the phone in my back pocket would work, huh?"

"Absolutely not. Now go have fun. At work." She wiggles her eyebrows.

"Can we skip to the good part? Where I'm eating at Top Shelf and not slogging through phone calls to alumni?" I'm both excited and terrified to go there.

I leave the room and am grateful to be heading out since Kenzie and Millie start oohing and aahing in an obnoxious way.

"Aren't you both late for work?" I say, glancing at my non-existent watch.

"Some of us have a more flexible schedule than others," Kenzie says, wagging her eyebrows behind Miles's back. I try to give her a silent threat, but she just grins wider.

Miles opens the door to his car for me and it takes me a moment to jumpstart my brain with the action. Maybe guys like Miles aren't only in fairytales and Hallmark movies.

I pull down the visor, opening the mirror, and start applying the limited amount of makeup I wear. I've never been the one to have time for the full face of makeup and I have no idea what contouring is. My mother stopped wearing makeup when my dad got sick, and I never had the desire to go almost full-costume makeup on a day-to-day basis. I like the simple routine of mascara, eye shadow and blush. It's easy whether I'm wearing my glasses or contacts.

It's only a couple minutes drive and I have to give him a couple directions to drop me off. My building isn't easily accessible from a parking lot.

"Thank you so much for the ride," I say, smiling at him. Dang, Miles has a great smile. And his lips are perfect. I just want to...

"Have a great day. Should I pick you up here?" he asks.

I think a moment. "Maybe over by the softball field? That isn't a far walk from where my last meeting is."

I get out of the car and watch him drive away. What would life be like to have a hunky guy drop me off for work every day?

CHAPTER 9
Miles

W hy is everything with Dani so effortless?

She didn't freak out at me because she needed four hours to get ready for the day. And she was genuinely grateful for the ride to work.

No matter what keeps coming up when I'm at my desk, I can't keep my mind off her. I go through the motions of work, checking through reports and doing what I can to listen in during meetings, but I keep turning over all the surprises Dani brings to the table.

The problem is, I think my mom knows something is up. And now I've been summoned to her office like I'm heading to death row. At least that's how her shy assistant makes it sound. It's a miracle the girl has stuck around as long as she has.

I knock three times on the door and stand, waiting for her permission to enter.

"Come in, son," she says, adjusting her glasses as she thumbs through several stacks of paper.

I take a seat in the wingback chair, the only office to have something so comfortable. I'd overheard my mom say it's to lull people into a sense of security before she puts them in their place.

That's why I don't scoot back fully, sitting on the front two-thirds of the chair.

"What do you need?" I ask, knowing I'm playing with fire by pressing. It's already getting close to time for me to pick up Dani.

"Did you get all those reports filed like we needed?" she asks, glancing up. She pulls off the glasses and stares at me.

I nod. "Yes, I did that last Friday."

"And what about the newest research wing? Have you figured out the details there?"

I take a deep breath and nod. "I'm going to dinner with one of our old investors tonight. He has all the contacts to get our newest heart rate machine research going."

There's a faint smile on her face when she says, "Good."

She doesn't dismiss me yet, which means there's something else on her mind.

"What about your plans for a plus one to the Investor's Ball?" And there it is, the first question about my relationship status today.

"Actually, I do have someone I'll be bringing."

My mother's lips pinch at the corners. "Please tell me it's not Amanda, or whatever your newest fling's name is."

It takes all I have to keep from grinning. I love my mother, but our relationship isn't as strong as, say Trey and his mother's. And it seems my plans to date random women have hit their mark.

"And what's this one's name?" she asks in resignation.

"Dani Higgins."

Her eyes blink a few times and I realize my misstep. "Danielle Higgins, but she likes going by Dani."

"I doubt her family is in any of our circles?" Mom tips her head back an inch, waiting for the response.

I frown. "You mean your circles?" The distinction is small, and by default of the nature of our business, I know a lot of people in the same places, but I'm not elitist. Another gift my father had given me.

"When you're ready, I'll reach out to Tanya."

"Good luck with that, Mom. Let me know how that goes, because I'm not getting back with her."

Mom rises from her chair and says, "You stubborn fool. She was the best thing that's ever happened to you. To us."

I blink several times and am surprised by the mental comparison my brain is giving me of Tanya and Dani.

"Then keep up the relationship for yourself. I don't want any part of it."

Sure, there are a lot of differences between my ex and my current fake girlfriend, but the one with long blonde hair is winning by a landslide. Not that there is any real contest because everything is just a business agreement between Dani and me, but it's nice to see that the Tanyas of the world aren't my only option. That's a definite eye-opener.

"Is there anything else *business-related* you need me to take care of?" If I draw the line in the sand now, maybe it will save me time standing here for the line of questioning.

Mom settles back into her desk and shakes her head. "You're dismissed."

Once I'm outside her office, I breathe in deeply, relishing the cooler air. And nothing has me more committed than the plan I've set in place with Dani.

CHAPTER 10

Dani

"A re you ready for this?" Miles asks, putting the car in drive. He is waiting for me once I get out of work and I'm not going to admit it out loud, but he's a sight for sore eyes, ones that have been staring at a screen all day.

"That all depends on what this dinner will entail. So the guy is a former investor in your company. We're meeting with him why?" I lean forward, trying to see in the dim light as I fix the makeup that didn't quite survive the hectic day. One of those bright light mirrors would be awesome right now.

The great thing is I have my makeup bag to do any touchups on our way to the restaurant.

Miles adjusts his hand on the steering wheel, looking out the window. "We were good friends in high school. He moved to the Czech Republic after graduating college to take over some family business his grandfather started."

I nod. "That's impressive. I can't imagine living anywhere other than Boston." To be honest, I wouldn't mind doing the traveling thing at some point. Traveling is my favorite hobby. I just wish my wallet didn't cry every time I want to book a trip.

"It's pretty cool over there. I flew over about three years ago to see him. Prague is amazing."

"I've seen pictures of Prague, but seeing it in person sounds idyllic." All the old castles and the expanses of countryside. I'd thought about heading over to do a backpacking tour in Europe, but student loans came calling a lot sooner than I could manage to put them off.

"So, I'll probably need to know some things about your childhood, or high school or whatever." I'm totally winning the awkwardness award for tonight. I'm more nervous than I thought I'd be for our first fake date. Because our walk around the Common wasn't a date. More like a business agreement.

"Childhood, huh? Maybe we'll start with the high school and college years first, just so you know the more recent parts of my life." One side of his lips tips up into a smile. I'm struck with how kissable they look right now. Perfectly formed and I can imagine them pressed against mine.

I need to think about something else. Wanting to kiss him might lead to other feelings and I can't afford a trip down Heartbreak Lane.

"You know I went to Boston University," he says. I'm over here picturing a make-out session and he's going along like there isn't an attraction pulling us together. Maybe I'm not cut out for this kind of thing. "That's where I met Jack and Spencer. Trey and I were good friends back in high school. Speaking of which, they already know about our arrangement."

I gasp and lean over to slap his arm, not with force. "You told them? That was one of the rules."

He chuckles and shakes his head. "They were the ones who convinced me to ask you. And you can't tell me you didn't say something to your roommates." When he turns to give me a teasing grin, I laugh.

"I've sworn Kenzie to secrecy, but I haven't told anyone else." I raise my hands as if I have nothing to hide.

He punches the gas, sending us hurtling around a car and back into the other lane. "Kenzie, huh? I would've thought it was Evie."

That sobers me a bit. "Yeah, she's the sweetest. I feel bad not telling her, but Kenzie gets me. And I told her on accident before remembering we weren't supposed to share." Circling back to his words I say, "Are your friends willing to keep it under wraps?"

"Yeah, but the deal is we'll have to do something with them. They're nosy like that."

I sit back, wondering what his friends would be like. Do they all wear incredibly nice suits and drive cars like this? If so, they are on a whole other level than what I'm used to.

"Do they all have girlfriends?" I ask, my curiosity getting the better of me.

"No, they don't, actually." A smile spreads over his face. "Maybe we should plan something and invite your roommates along."

I laugh, wondering why he'd gone to that extreme. "I appreciate the gesture, but this is fake, remember? You're probably not going to want us all hanging on for dear life when this ends, right?"

His expression sobers and a pang of regret hits my chest. "Sorry, I didn't mean it like—"

With a raised hand, he cuts me off. "No, it's all good. I just like hanging out with you, to be honest. You don't have expectations to be at the biggest parties and meet celebrities. At least, that's the impression I've gotten so far."

It takes a few seconds for his words to seep in. "I mean, if you're offering, I'll meet Matt Damon or John Krasinski. Chris Evans lives here in town somewhere, right?" There's silence in the car before I finally crack a smile. "I'm just teasing."

Miles blows out a breath. "Okay, for a second there, I thought about turning the car around and dropping you off at home."

"Probably best not to. I don't need to make this relationship, or fake relationship the shortest ever."

"What's your longest relationship?" Miles asks, giving me a small smile as he turns to look at me while slowing down at a stop light.

"Five and a half years."

He gives a low whistle and stares at me with wide eyes. "That's like a marathon in relationship terms, right?"

"Oh you know, the typical high school sweethearts making it about three years and five months through college until he breaks up with me after Christmas break during our senior year."

Miles urges the car forward as the light turns green. "Wait, didn't you just graduate a few weeks ago?"

I nod. "Yep. Then my next relationship was all of three weeks and you saw how that one ended."

"Dumpster fire. I get it. But I think we're both better off without the two of them. Amber wanted to go to my friend Trey's birthday bash instead of to The Riptide that night. I was planning to take her after dinner. Trey is a good guy, but his food palate is like a four-year-old."

"Chicken nuggets, fries, and hot dogs?" I ask, thinking of one of the kids Millie nannies for. I helped her one day a few weeks ago and that was the rolling menu for the day.

Miles points at me and says, "Exactly. And then there's the selection of alcohol that eats up his paycheck for one game. A guy needs real fuel before entering a place like that."

"I thought hockey players don't drink or anything during the season."

"He doesn't, but he always says he has to keep up his reputation as a great party thrower." Miles pulls up to the curb and I'm trying to be patient since the entrance to the parking garage is another block ahead of us.

We're almost directly across the street from where we'd met Sunday. My door opens by a guy in uniform and Miles walks around the car, handing the man the keys.

Miles reaches out and grabs my hand, causing my fingers to tingle and my heart to give a little jump at the fact I'm here at one of the nicest restaurants in town, dressed in clothes that both look fashionable and are comfy, and I didn't get sweaty taking the T or walking after finding parking.

But we're a few steps in when my body recognizes I'm wearing heels and homes in on that fact. My left heel gets caught in a crack in the sidewalk but I'm able to pull it free with a quick pull. It's only then that the right ankle aborts the mission and I've got the ground in my sights. Just before I land, I feel strong arms around me.

"I told Evie I'm not trained in heels." I glance around and we're posed as if he's dipping me in the middle of a dance.

"Maybe you should invest in some wedges. Height without the wobbly factor?" The smile on Miles's face is soft, and a swarm of bees take flight in my stomach. Maybe this fake dating thing is a bad idea. In fact, a quick check of my heart tells me that I'm in trouble.

I laugh and shake my head. "How did you know that?"

He sighs and I can see the far off look in his eyes. "I too had a long relationship that ended in early winter. She was into everything fashion. And I heard a lot about it daily."

He pulls me to a standing position, and I give him a smile. "Thanks for saving me. And I'm sorry about your girlfriend. Or ex." She must be the one I've seen a hundred pictures of.

With a shoulder shrug, he says, "It's over. We'll survive, right?"

As an attendant opens the door to the restaurant, I breathe out, "I hope so."

CHAPTER 11
Miles

Sure, this was a gutsy move to bring Dani. But I already had to meet up with Oliver about backing a research project we want to start at the company and figured this would be a good time to test things out with her.

And getting to know her so far has been worthwhile. I'd meant what I said about feeling comfortable around her. I didn't have to put on a certain expression or be uptight about things in her presence.

Something in her face gives off the vulnerability I feel ever since Tanya broke up with me. Maybe we'll be able to help each other.

"Two for the Clark reservation," I tell the hostess.

"I have you down for three," she says, glancing up at me again.

I nod. "He should be here any minute." With a quick glance around the lobby, I don't see Oliver anywhere.

"Already here," says a familiar voice from behind.

I turn to find Ollie's smile stretched from ear to ear. "It's good to see you again, friend."

"You too," he says after a back-slapping hug. We step back and his eyes go to Dani at my side.

"Ollie, this is Dani. My girlfriend." I have to hold back a grin

67

as I see how that one word transforms Dani's expression into shock.

Ollie steps up and shakes her hand. "It's about time he found someone semi-normal."

Dani laughs. "You've got the semi right. But what makes you say that?"

Ollie gives a quick shrug. "Just a lot of experience being around this guy. And you're not wearing a sour expression, glancing around for someone better to speak to."

Turning to me, Dani gives me a side-eye. "If he can tell all that within five seconds of meeting, that's a problem."

We all laugh as the hostess leads us to our table, and I make sure to help Dani into her seat. She looks up and gives me a soft, "Thank you," before picking up the menu. It's small, but something about that act of gratitude takes over, sending a warm sensation throughout my chest.

It doesn't take long for Ollie and me to decide what to get, while Dani pours over every inch of the menu. While her head is down, Ollie grins at me, giving me a thumbs up. His opinion is a big deal, as he's been one of those people who's kept me grounded over the years.

The server takes our order, and we settle into conversation.

"So, Dani, how'd this guy snag you?" Oliver says, pointing at me.

She glances over, her eyes shining with mischief. "Well, we were on separate dates when we found my date and his date in the men's room making out."

Ollie's eyebrows are practically in his hairline. "Are you serious? What a story starter."

I laugh. "It gets better. She threw Dr Pepper all over me, thinking I was her date."

Leaning in, Ollie says, "If I were a writer, that would be the perfect meet cute."

I raise an eyebrow. "When did my science-loving friend become a romantic?"

Ollie takes a sip of his drink and smiles. "I dated a writer for a few months. It's interesting the pains people will endure for their art, you know? All the crazy hours of chasing inspiration and hoping that the words will come. I'd rather stick to facts and numbers."

The three of us laugh.

"So are you dating anyone now?" I ask, curious as to what he's been up to since I went radio silent after my breakup.

Oliver shakes his head. "Not at the moment. I'm actually back in the states for a while, looking at the chances to expand the family business here."

I nod, liking the sound of that. Not only would I have the chance to see him more, but we'd be able to do some business here and there.

"What is it you do?" Dani asks. She takes a sip of water from her glass, but waits for Oliver's response.

"My grandfather started a cell phone company in the Czech Republic about thirty years ago when they were like bricks. We've come a long way since then, but the company has expanded into several other markets and tech products. I'm more interested in the tech than the phones, to be honest."

Dani nods, looking fully invested. Another contrast to how Tanya had been with my friends. "Is there anything I've heard of?"

Oliver sits back, his eyes narrowing as he takes her in. He glances in my direction, the small raise of his eyebrows and widening of his smile tells me he whole-heartedly approves of Dani. And while this is technically a fake relationship, I hope we'll end up friends even after, even though a niggling feeling tells me I'm swimming in deep waters.

"We've made several brands of ear buds for PopCandy, as well as other wearable gear."

"My brother went to London on a business trip a couple weeks ago and brought me home some of those ear buds," Dani says grinning.

Oliver leans forward again and asks, "What was he doing in London?"

I realize I'm intrigued as well because Dani and I haven't gotten into the specifics of family and siblings yet. I don't have any, but now I know she has a brother.

"He works for a real estate company based there. They opened up a couple branches here over the past few years, but Landon is their traveling consultant."

Oliver's eyes narrow. "I'm going to go out on a limb and name drop the only real estate company I know in London. He wouldn't happen to work for the Hamilton Group, would he?"

Dani's eyes go wide, and I love the look of surprise on her face. I mean like, not love. Because we're going to be friends after this relationship. We'd just need to get an apartment and a few more people who constantly drop by and we could make our own sitcom. The one where Miles and Dani end their fake relationship.

She nods. "That's the one. I went with him on their cruise a couple months ago."

"The owner, Roman, is one of my good friends. We were in the same fraternity in college."

At the mention of Roman, I nod. "I've met him a few times. He's a good guy."

"Imagine how small the world is," Dani says, grinning as she lifts her water glass once again.

Our food comes and we chat here and there throughout the meal.

"I seriously can't believe how good this is," Dani says, groaning as she puts another bite of the Tuscan Chicken into her mouth. "I might have to look for a copycat recipe and make it."

I open my mouth to ask the question that follows that, but clamp it shut, knowing I should know that much.

"You like to cook?" Oliver asks, and I give an inward sigh, grateful he asked it.

She tips her head back and forth for a few seconds, finishing the bite. "It depends on my mood. I've been branching out from the ten recipes my mother made growing up, thanks to the internet. I'm not ready to be the chef of my own restaurant. Yet."

I laugh. "I don't think many people are."

"Definitely not me. I think I make a better food critic," Oliver says, adjusting the napkin on his lap.

"Not a chance. I don't think I've heard you criticize food. Ever," I say.

"Probably true. I love food, okay? So, Miles, what did you want to meet about?" Oliver says, wiping off his mouth with the cloth napkin and sitting back with his glass of wine.

With how well the evening has gone so far, I've almost forgotten why we're here in the first place.

"Our company is starting research on some better equipment for the hospitals. Given the rise in flu cases that hits every fall, we need to find a technology that is smaller and can be multipurposed depending on the capacities and needs of the hospitals."

Oliver grins. "And you want me to work on it?"

I run a hand through my hair and think through the correct words I want to convey. "You're my number one option, but if you're busy, we'd accept anything you can give."

He turns to Dani and laughs. "The guy is just here for my money."

"No, it's not that—"

Oliver laughs. "I know, man. You could fund this with your pocket change. Let me get in touch with my assistant and see what my schedule looks like. When are you wanting to get started?"

"In the next few weeks. My mother wants to have a prototype rolling out by September so we can start sending them to hospitals."

The expression on his face sobers and he looks over at Dani before settling his gaze on me. "Still working under Mama Clark, huh?"

I sigh, turning my focus to Dani who's staring at me with

curiosity brimming. "For the time being, yes. She keeps saying she'll retire and then pushes everything back with another idea. Except this one came from me."

Oliver takes the check from the server and sticks his card in there.

I reach over to try and insert my own. "No, no," he says. "I've got this one."

Pointing to myself, I say, "I'm the one who invited you to dinner for business."

"I got to the check first." Oliver's smile is triumphant and I relent.

We stand up after he gets his card back and Dani excuses herself to the restroom.

"I don't know how you found someone like her, but keep her close, man." Oliver slaps me on the back a couple times as we weave toward the front of the restaurant.

I swallow, wondering if I should confess our true standing. Oliver has always been a good friend, one of those I can pick up and talk with whenever. But something keeps me from saying anything.

Probably the praise he has for Dani.

Since my father's death, I've been under the scrutiny of my mother, who's always been in CEO mode. It's times like this that I miss my father's input in life things.

"That's what I'm going for," I say, holding out my hands to emphasize it. "I'm just good at picking women who use me to rise the ladder in the family business and then move on."

That's what Tanya had done.

"Does Dani work with you?" Oliver asks, tucking his wallet into his back pocket.

I shake my head. "She's a development person over at Boston University."

"So she's in research?" The confusion on Oliver's face has me going through everything Dani has told me about her job.

"No, she plans mixers and parties for alumni, I guess." I turn to search for Dani after I say that, knowing, as her boyfriend, I should know details like that.

"I don't know," Oliver says. "Dani is different from everything I've seen."

I smile, seeing her weave through several tables to get back to where we stand. "Yeah, she is."

It's not something I'm ready to accept, but there is something about Dani that makes me want to plan for the future. Even though, given our agreement, that should be the furthest thing from my mind.

She makes it seem like I'm finally breathing fresh air after being trapped in the same room for decades.

"Ready?" she asks, slipping her hand to hold onto my elbow gently.

We step out of the restaurant and Oliver takes her free hand in his, leaning over it. He's about to kiss it and my defenses rise, making me want to strangle the guy.

Ollie glances at me and straightens. I doubt I've seen a bigger grin from him. "That's what I thought."

Dani's head swivels back and forth between us and I take in a deep breath, trying to figure out how to bridge this situation. Because Dani is curious and she's going to ask what this was after Ollie leaves.

"Thank you for a wonderful evening," Oliver says, raising a hand to wave. "I have to head back to my hotel and get ready for a big day of travel tomorrow. Good luck and I'll let you know what I find out, Miles."

He waves and turns to leave.

Dani sighs next to me and leans in a bit more. "That was fun."

I laugh and nod. "Yeah, it was, wasn't it? What do you want to do now?"

She yawns then. "As much as I would love to continue to hang out, I think I need to get to bed. I've been up way too late planning this mixer so my boss doesn't freak out."

I nod, leading her over to the valet station and handing one of the attendants the ticket. "Okay, Cinderella. We'll get you home before midnight."

She laughs and I watch her profile, knowing that each moment I spend with her is making it harder to remember this isn't real.

CHAPTER 12
Dani

T op Shelf was everything I could've imagined and more. The food was incredible, the ambience swanky, and meeting Oliver had been my second favorite time of the evening.

The first was definitely the doorstep drop-off. It's been so long since I've actually been taken to the door by a date that having Miles stand next to me on the stoop gave me a shot of that feeling when you have a new crush.

The part that surprises me the most though, was Oliver's admission that Miles hasn't had the best streak in his dating life. Then again, he dated Amber, so that should have been a huge clue right there. Miles has been every bit the gentleman, and it makes me wonder if he's dated the women he has because they are the only ones he's ever known, or if that is just his default setting.

A huge part of me hopes it's the former.

Fake relationship. What part of that does my brain not comprehend?

I'm at work on Wednesday morning, trying to wade through the list of other alumni to invite to the mixer. And all I can do is think back to the night before.

It's been three days since we began our arrangement, and my

heart didn't get the memo that it's all fake. But everything Miles does gets analyzed on loop, wondering if men like him are made in a factory somewhere and kept hidden from women like me or what.

He hasn't flaunted his wealth in extreme ways. When Clay bought his Mustang during our freshman year of college, it took at least six months for him to acknowledge that he was always trying to get the conversation on his car. Add that to the red flags I should've counted long ago.

And Miles opens every door and pulls out chairs for me every time we've gone anywhere.

I mean, the guy is making it hard to remember this is all fake. It could've just been on my end, but his hug at the end of the night had been charged with all the good feelings, meaning my stomach was basically taking off for space with all the excitement.

"Dani," my boss's voice calls from the desktop phone on my desk.

I jump, wondering how long I'd been daydreaming, and pick up the receiver. "Yes, Sharon?"

"How's it coming? I haven't seen any new names on the guest list."

I grimace, trying to keep my irritation under control. "I did manage to get one of Boston's richest bachelors, though."

Silence for several seconds and then Sharon says, "Miles Clark is a good find, but we need more like him." She pauses and says, "He's never been to any of our events before. How did you manage that?"

She makes him seem like some ogre who'd rather stay holed up in a forest lodge than communicate with people. And yet, I've found he's more the opposite.

"We've met a few times and I happened to convince him." More like negotiate with his strange request. But that's beside the point.

"Good work. Let me know if you can get any others. We need to have some more names to get people into the party."

For some reason, the image of people standing outside the doors to the arena, as if waiting for the Black Friday shopping sales to commence pops into my mind.

"Will do, Sharon."

I press the button to end the call and dial the next number, trying to smile as I listen to the dial tone. I'm still not convinced the fake happiness works like people say because I'm already sick of calling people. There's got to be a better way.

The caller doesn't answer and I put the phone down, deciding to search in my internet browser for something more efficient.

Miles: How's work going?

I smile like a schoolgirl when I see the text from Miles.

Me: It's Wednesday and I'm still breathing. So, I would say I'm alive. How are you today?

Miles: You might want to check out this link.

It doesn't come through in a quick amount of time, so I type out:

Are you trying to commit fraud with my bank accounts?

The link comes through after and then a large smiley emoji appears on my screen.

Miles: I'm not sure you're the type to fall for those, are you?

Swoon goes my heart. Focus, Dani. Fake relationship.

Me: Of course, I am. I mean, I almost clicked on a link to my bank the other day. But my mom had that happen a year ago and the bank had to replace fifteen grand.

Miles: Oh wow. Does your mom live close?

I bite my lip, knowing I need to get work done while I'm on the clock. But I really like talking to Miles. He gives me a good shot of serotonin.

Me: Yeah, over in Brookline.

Miles: Mine is in Belmont.

Me: Does your dad live there too?

We hadn't gotten to the specifics of family at all, and I'm more than curious.

Seconds tick by and I worry that I've said something wrong.

Miles: He passed away about three years ago. Heart attack.

And now I'm sorry we're doing this over text. I type out a message and then click the delete button a bunch of times.

This needs a phone call.

I press the dial tone and several rings pass before I hear his voice come on the line.

"Sorry, are you busy?"

Noise in the background tells me he is, but a few seconds later, it's silent.

"Just got out of a work meeting."

I have no idea if his days are busy, and if he can even talk. Then again, why would he want to chat away with his fake girlfriend? Probably to get more information to solidify our story. That's what my brain can come up with on short notice.

"I just wanted to call and say I'm sorry about your dad. I probably should've waited to ask you in person."

"No, you're fine," he says, his voice just a hint deeper, almost sounding like he's getting choked up.

I blow out a breath, doing what I do best in awkward situations. Talk.

"My dad died too, when I was almost in high school. He had a lot of health problems, but cancer ended up taking him."

"Was that hard?" Miles asks. "I mean, for you and your brother?"

"My mom had a hard time for a while, but my brother helped take care of her and work at our grandfather's company. I ended up being the go-to babysitter for my younger sisters."

"You have more siblings?" His surprise makes me laugh.

"Three younger sisters. We lived with one and a half bathrooms, so there was always drama at our house. But I loved it."

Several seconds of quiet hit me and I pull the phone back to check that the line hasn't been disconnected.

"I always wanted siblings. My dad said it was hard enough for my mom to take time off work to have me."

"Did they work together?"

"Yes, my dad had the idea and started it before they married, but she took it and ran with it, making it into the company it is today."

Corporate mother. I'd have to keep that in mind when we meet. That helps the image Oliver gave me when he talked about Miles still working under "Mama Clark."

"Sounds like she's put a lot of work into it," I say.

"She's great at business," he says. "There are times when I wish she could leave work at the office though. You know, so we could act like mother and son when I'm home."

The longing in his voice has me wondering what it would've been like to grow up as an only child. Some of my best memories come from the experiences of dealing with and loving siblings. I would've had to move home for the last semester of college if Landon hadn't come to live with me.

"We have a monthly game night if you want to join. I mean, then you'll realize having siblings can be trouble." We're fake dating and here I am inviting him to family functions.

My family would love him, but I don't need to get ahead of myself. The poor guy will probably be grateful to be rid of me by the end of this.

He chuckles and says, "That sounds like it would be fun. I'm not the best at games, though. Are you all overly intense and should I expect a fight to break out?"

I laugh, thinking of the last game night we had just a few weeks ago. I'd invited my new roommates and the competitive natures in all of them came out. "No fist fights, just friendly banter."

"Just tell me when." There is a pause and he says, "Oh, did you check that link I sent?"

I pull my phone away and put him on speaker, searching for the message screen. With a click on the link, it pulls up to a page on the internet and there's a picture of me falling into Miles's arms just outside Top Shelf.

I scan the article, and the caption underneath the picture says, "Miles Clark out on the town with new unknown girl."

When my brain refocuses on the present, I realize Miles is talking again.

"I mean, are you okay?" His voice is soft and tender, making me like the guy that much more. As a friend, obviously. I can commit to being friends after this.

After an internal examination, my stomach is tight, and I have to walk over to the window at the edge of my cubicle just to make sure no one is out there right now. "I'm kind of freaking out. Why?"

"What's got you scared?"

Oh, I don't know, Miles, the way I'm looking at you in this picture like you're my hero after saving my life from the cement below. Or that someone managed to get a picture of that moment and now has it plastered all over the city. Awesome.

I blow out a breath. "I'm good at staying under the radar, so I guess it's surprising to have my face on the front page of the Boston Globe." I mean, I was on the front page of the Life section back in the day for taking third place in my fifth-grade spelling bee. That picture I knew was being taken. This one definitely not.

"I'm so sorry, Dani," he says, sounding tired. "I can usually spot the paparazzi a mile away. Next time we go out, I'll make sure to focus on that."

"It's okay. I mean, that's just what we'll have to figure out for the next few weeks." Not that having cameras in my face sounds ideal. "We have to kind of sell our relationship, so your mom doesn't bug you, right?"

When he speaks again, he sounds a lot farther away. "If at any point you feel uncomfortable, please let me know."

"Will do." And then the thought comes to me that this is his daily life. When we'd looked up pictures with Kenzie, there had been thousands, if not millions. "How do you deal with it all the time?"

He chuckles a bit. "It's not as new to me as it is for you. I mean, I've been in newspapers and gossip columns since I was around ten. At this point, I ignore most of it."

"I'll have to remember that for next time." Please let there not be a next time.

"Okay, when do you want to go on your shopping spree?" he chuckles and the pinch of anxiety in my chest eases up slightly.

I glance at the calendar I pulled up on my screen to verify delivery dates of the décor for the mixer. "Well, this week will be better than next. I'll be trying to put everything together for the mixer and I might be zoned into that for most of the week."

"Lucky for you I don't have anything big I need to attend next week. How about Friday?"

I nod to myself. "That should work. I have a meeting with my division until three-thirty, but I can be ready to go after that."

"I'll pick you up at Boston University then. Plan on 3:35."

I smile and say, "Count on it. But I have to warn you, I'm the worst shopper ever. Like, I usually buy things and take them home so I don't have to try them on, lack-of-patience type. I might need sustenance halfway through."

Miles laughs and says, "I'll buy you some pretzel bites and hold them out to nudge you along."

I let out a laugh and say, "I think you just read my mind. Don't forget the cheese!"

"Cheese it is," he says, letting out a low rumble of a laugh. "Once Sonia gets your measurements, it's a lot easier to get things fitted in the future."

"What happens if you gain weight in between fittings?" I'm being annoying right now, but having someone fit me with the right styles and sizes is something I've never experienced.

"Then, you just retake the measurements."

I sigh. "That sounds awful."

"Taking measurements isn't like running an Iron Man Race, Dani," he says with humor in his voice.

I glance around the room and say, "So what you're saying is I should probably go down all the ice cream and cookies we have on hand before this. Challenge accepted."

He lets out a groan and I can picture him rolling his eyes. "No, I'm just saying Sonia is used to retaking measurements. I've had to do it at least every year since all my growth spurts."

An image of a younger Miles parades through my mind. Was he the gangly kind? No, he probably turned heads even when he was younger.

"Okay, don't worry. I won't eat myself into a coma. See you then."

We hang up and my little laugh turns into a small cry. The guy is nearly perfect and I am far from it. I doubt I'll be able to come out of this situation with my heart intact.

CHAPTER 13

Miles

I t's been a couple years since I've been out to my alma mater, and here I am for the second time in a week. I smile as I remember telling my mother I was turning down a chance at Harvard to go to Boston University.

The Ivy League school had been my mother's goal for me since I was in diapers. And as I'd grown up in the shadow of her company and her presence in the society of Boston, I'd wanted to do something to get her attention. Going to a public school had done it. But she spent the next several weeks giving me the silent treatment because of it.

And now that I piece that together, Tanya did the same thing. If she was angry, it was up to me to "care enough" and ask all sorts of questions to mend our relationship. Not that Dani and I've had anything to argue about, but I wonder how she reacts when she disagrees.

Despite my mother's anger, I'd graduated Summa Cum Laude. But even that accomplishment was overshadowed by the fact I "could do that at a better school."

Me: I'm here.

My text is short, but I have a strange excitement pooling in my stomach at the idea of seeing Dani again. There aren't many places to park along this area, but with the directions I'd given to her to meet near the back of the university, she should be able to find me.

"Hey! I had no idea this was still part of the campus." Dani's smile is wide. She adjusts a large backpack over her shoulders.

"And you look like you're ready to head to a study group," I say, reaching out for the backpack. I open the door for her and then secure her backpack in the back seat.

"Well, I did just get out of college a few weeks ago. Old habits and all that." She turns to me and her eyes narrow. "How long ago did you graduate?"

"Undergrad or grad degree?"

Dani makes a face. "Of course you went back to get a masters. Either."

I chuckle and secure my seatbelt before we head out. "My undergrad was five years ago, and my business masters was three years ago."

Dani leans her head back against the headrest and closes her eyes. "Going back to school sounds like torture."

I nod. "It was. But that's over now. What are you? Twenty-two?"

"Didn't your mother ever tell you not to ask a woman her age?" Dani says, placing her hand over her chest in dismay. It takes a second for me to realize she's kidding.

With a shake of my head, I say, "That was all in my father's jurisdiction. And I might as well know, just in case someone happens to ask."

She smiles and says, "I'm two months away from twenty-three. My mom worried about me being a summer birthday and held me back a year in kindergarten."

I pull into the garage of Copley Place, a large mall near the Back Bay. "Throwing it all the way back to kindergarten, huh?"

"Yeah, I'm a summer birthday and had a lovely speech impediment at the time. She figured I could use another year to grow out of it."

I park and turn to her. "I never would've guessed."

"That's the beauty of bribes. I cashed in on every one my parents set out so I'd practice. I got the pink bike with the streamers out of the handlebars, a trip to the circus, and several new toys." She nods, her expression serious like she was one of the cool kids.

It's hard for me to keep my smile under control, as I'm trying to get the words out in a somber manner. "Pink streamers? I would've taken you for a neon green kind of girl."

She shakes her head. "Neon green is from my later, rebel days."

The two of us start laughing. As fun as she is, she seems like a rule follower and I'm sure the worst thing she's ever done was prank call someone.

"We're going here?" Dani asks, glancing through the window. The car sits facing out of the parking garage and the large buildings that make up the mall.

I can't tell by the look on her face whether it's a good thing or not. "Yeah, is that okay?"

She nods. "My friends and I went window shopping here once, but even the accessories were more than I could ever afford."

I park the car and turn to her. "This is the only place I know. And Sonia is one of the best at her job." We get out of the car and my phone rings for what feels like the hundredth time today.

"Give me one second," I say, seeing Oliver's name on the screen.

"Hey Ollie," I say, taking a few steps away from the car. Pacing is what I do when I talk on the phone.

"Hey yourself," he says, sounding like he's standing in front of a wind turbine. "I've just spoken with my assistant. I can give you a month to work on the project. Grandpa needs me back at the end of July for a couple weeks but I'm hoping that will be enough time to get your project underway."

I fist pump and say, "Thank you, Oliver. That means a lot."

"Oh don't worry. I'll be calling you for a favor soon enough." Oliver laughs and I follow.

"That's fine with me. I'm happy to reciprocate."

"I've got to run. See you next week."

We hang up the phone and I turn to Dani. My research project is going to be in good hands with Oliver, and I get to spend more time with Dani, which has been the bright spot of my week.

I turn to her, reaching out my hand to take hers. It's not a necessity to hold hands, but I tell myself the paparazzi are everywhere.

"Are you ready to do some shopping?"

CHAPTER 14
Dani

"We can always go to TJ Maxx. Or Ross. I'm a good bargain hunter," I say. My nerves are shaking like I'm about to walk onto a stage facing hundreds of people.

Miles laughs. "It's fine. Sonia will help you get set up with everything you need."

"Please tell me she won't torture me with high heels," I say, mostly to get a reaction out of him. "Unless you want your girl-friend to look like the damsel in distress type. I mean, fake girl-friend." I have to whisper the last part because people are approaching.

It gets the desired laugh and he says, "We can talk to her about non-heel options."

I should be excited about getting a few things for my wardrobe, but guilt is the overruling emotion here. He shouldn't be spending money on me when I'm not his real girlfriend. And I am definitely underdressed for this place. They're going to look at me like I walked in dressed in the styles from the past decade.

And to that I would say they'd be wrong, because who knows when or if my style has ever been popular.

We enter a large department store, and as if they have been

keeping watch, a couple of women in matching blue pants suits come scurrying over to us.

"Mr. Clark," one of the women fawns. "What a pleasure it is to have you in today."

Miles gives them what I've come to know as his business smile as he shifts from one foot to the other.

"Hello," he says, placing a hand on my lower back. A tingle travels all the way up my spine because of it. "I asked for Sonia to be here today," he says, his tone firm.

The one woman's face falls a bit. "Of course, I'll call her up here." As she and the other woman hurry away, I lean closer to Miles. The smell of his cologne is different than any other I've smelled before. Right now, if he told me where he bought it from, I might just go get a bottle to spray on my pillow. Okay, so I would wait for him to not be here. I don't need him thinking he's in a fake relationship with a stalker type.

"Does this happen to you often? The attention and the hurrying to fulfill your request?" I ask, glancing up at him. He's probably five or so inches taller than me, but from this close, it's like I'm seeing a whole other side of him.

He nods, looking somber. "Yeah, more than I'd like. It's a casualty of the business."

"They act intimidated, like you're some kind of tyrant."

"That's because I'm the son of Anita Clark. She strikes that kind of fear into people." He looks at me and says, "Are you okay?"

"I mean, it's a little crazy," I say, crossing my eyes in an attempt to help him relax. I also put that detail about his mother into my memory vault. The woman sounds scary.

He chuckles. "It has its perks. I mean, I don't have to worry about waiting too long when I go to familiar places."

"I assume this is like the paparazzi? Has it been this way your whole life?" I ask. Getting stared at wherever I go would be a big drawback of being rich.

"Not my whole life. I think that's why my dad started

Gentleman Prep, so I would be trained in all the things I needed to survive life."

I frown and try to figure out if I've missed something. "What do you mean?" I ask. "Your dad wasn't a schoolteacher, was he? I thought you said he'd started the business before meeting your mom."

Miles chuckles and shakes his head. "No, not a teacher. He just wanted me to be a decent guy. With all the things to learn in business, he was worried I wouldn't understand some of the important manners. So, we would have a small lesson every week that he called Gentlemen Prep. We would work on things like etiquette and opening doors for women and stuff like that. My friend Jack usually came for those."

There's definitely a factory where this man was made. I'm pretty sure my mouth has been hanging open for most of the conversation.

Everything that had to do with manners in the Higgins family came from our mother, not that our dad was bad about it, but he often worked until late in the evening, unless we had a game or a concert. It's interesting to note that the things I've been impressed with from Miles came from the time spent with his father.

"What?" he asks.

"That's really cool. I mean, my dad was working a lot and we got along, but it was my mom who did most of the training in our house." Heat rises to my cheeks. "And I have to say I probably didn't listen to the instructions as well as I should've. When you meet Mama Higgins, don't blame her for that."

He laughs loud and long. "I think I'd like to meet her. I can imagine she's got as much spunk as you."

A woman hustles up to us looking to be in her mid-forties. "Mr. Clark," she says, walking up with her hand outstretched. "What a pleasure to have you here today. I was just finishing up the last few items for your summer order. Is there something else you need?" She hasn't made eye contact with me yet, but Miles turns attention to me.

"We need to get a few things for my girlfriend," he says with a whisper of a smile on his lips.

He just said girlfriend. Cue the internal scream of excitement as the sound of his voice goes in a loop in my brain. Clay had always avoided calling me his girlfriend, probably to look for better options.

Red flag four hundred and ninety-six.

The woman finally glances over at me and to her credit, her expression doesn't change. No expression of disgust, no frown.

"Perfect. I've got the list of your upcoming events. Do you want me to follow those while fitting?"

"Yes. That will work. She'll also need a few casual outfits, for any random meetings and for her job."

I squeeze his arm and make him turn to look up at me. "How many events are we planning here, sir?" I whisper as Sonia heads up to the counter to get a tape measure.

"I'd rather have you prepared for whatever comes," he says. The half-smile he gives me sends my heart racing.

I laugh nervously. "Well, if this is what you do for your fake girlfriend," I say, dropping my voice to whisper, "I wonder what it would be like to be your actual girlfriend."

And now to usher in the embarrassment.

My hands are waving and my eyes are bug-eyed at this point, wishing I could take back what I'd just said. I don't want him to think that I am after him for his money.

"I didn't mean it like that," I say. "I just meant for us, as friends, this is kind of a lot."

His expression shifts from somber to a smile with the word friend.

"Do you think of us as friends?" The words are low and they do something to the walls I've built around my heart. Like a tiny earthquake that's setting up for the big one to come along and knock everything down.

"Yes," I say. "I mean, we've been through what feels like battle together with our mutual break-up date. You also introduced me to one of your good friends at a really nice restaurant. So I kind of feel like we're friends, but I mean, if you don't want me to refer to us that way—"

It's his turn to wave his hands, and he rests them on my upper arms, sending a shiver running down my spine. "No, I like it. You haven't been the one begging me for things, and we talk just like friends, like true friends."

His words hit me and I say, "Is it really that hard to figure out who your real friends are?"

"Yeah," he says, his voice more tender than I'm used to. He gives me a sad smile. "Let's just say friends who want to listen to your problems and help you out with nothing in return are hard to come by when your last name is Clark."

On instinct, I wrap my arms around his waist and pull him into a hug. Probably not the best spot for this in a clothing store, but the poor guy needs it. And we're fake dating, so a little PDA in this situation isn't all bad. That's the story I'm sticking to because he smells that dang good.

"So how did you meet your other friends? The ones who told you about the fake dating thing?" I keep my cheek pressed against the nice suit coat he's wearing, wondering if this is the one I spilled Dr Pepper on or not. The details from that night aren't all crisp and clear.

It takes a moment to realize he's rubbing circles on my back as he thinks about my question. I'm here for it.

"Some of them run in the same social circle, or their parents have with my mom, and others we just met at random things. But it's taken a long time to get to where we are and I'm grateful for them."

I smile feeling an ache in my chest. I hadn't had a lot of good friends since Clay and I started dating. He was kind of a time suck and most of my friends had moved on after spending months trying to get me to come out with them. But ever since I've moved into the Spice House, I've been able to find common ground and a lot of fun with each roommate.

Sonia waves for us to follow to a set of dressing rooms and pulls out her tape measure. I thought we'd go inside one of the rooms and I'd have to shed my clothing, but she starts taking measurements of my chest, calling them out to a woman behind us poised with a tablet.

As she works to adjust the tape measure around my chest area, I have to avoid looking at Miles. I am not overly well endowed, but neither am I an A-cup. I'd rather the focus not be there at the moment.

My best weapon of defense at this point is thinking of Miles as my brother Landon. Obviously there's no worries about falling in love with a brother, but Miles is still too hot to completely wipe the attraction from my brain.

"Will you be requiring new underthings?" Sonia asks, looking up at me.

I blurt out, "No," at the same time Miles says, "Yes."

I turn to glare at him, trying to channel the fact that he does not need to buy me underwear. But he's not paying attention to me at all.

"I recommend it," Sonia says, folding up her tape measure. "The bra you're wearing right now is too small in the cup area. See how it squeezes right here and spills over—"

"Okay, let's do it," I say, cutting her off. I'm pretty sure I look like I've got a sunburn from the heat scorching my face. Nothing like a woman to point directly at the area I don't want to emphasize to make the embarrassment surge.

Sonia nods. "Okay, we'll start over here with the bras and underwear and move onto the casual attire. From there we can try on some formal gowns and shoes to finish it off. Is there a budget?"

I freeze as the woman looks at me. I'm pretty sure the only thing I could afford is her tape measure.

"No budget. Make her feel comfortable." Miles takes a few steps to follow as we head to the lingerie section before I whirl around and give him my most serious glare.

"I'm sorry to do this to you, since you've been most gracious with this whole adventure, but this is one part of the tour you're not allowed to see," I say.

I hear a light laugh behind me and turn to see Sonia grinning. "Miles, I've got that selection of new clothing ready for you to check over. Why don't you head to the men's section and I'll have Carl start tailoring the suits? You can rejoin us when you're done."

Miles smiles, raising his hands in the air. "Point taken. I'll give you some privacy, babe." He takes a step forward and leans down. What is with this guy's superpower to make me an immovable statue? I stand there as the suspense rises, his lips inching closer to mine. But instead of connecting, he turns, kissing me on the cheek.

I suck in a deep breath, surprised by the wildfire spreading across my cheek from the contact. And why am I disappointed there was no lip action?

"OK." I watch him walk away, as if seeing him for the first time. So much for all the vault walls I've tried to set up. The man is breaking those down like Thor with his hammer, Mjolnir.

I turn over the tags on the lacy bra and do my best not to choke at the price tag.

"Well done, dear," Sonia says giving me a warm smile.

I point in the direction where Miles disappeared and say, "For pushing him away?"

"So it's good to have some surprises for later. It keeps a relationship rolling." She winks at me and suddenly I can't breathe.

"Um, no, that's not why I didn't want him following me over here," I say, my face hot with embarrassment. "It's just that... this is a lot all at once."

"He's definitely a catch, but it seems you're good for him," Sonia says with a smile as she thumbs through the racks of brassieres.

I laugh and say, "I don't know about that." The confusion on her face reminds me that this relationship is supposed to be believable for the world and I hurry to amend it. "I mean, he's always been a gentleman to me. I'm still trying to figure out what he sees in me."

Sonia hands me a couple bras in different colors and moves onto the tables of lacy underwear. "Probably something different than the other women he's dated."

"Have you known him long?" My curiosity is what's gotten me to this point in life and I might as well embrace the chance to know more about Miles.

She reaches forward and pats my hand. "Oh honey, I've known him since he was born. I've been his mother's personal shopper since her first big board meeting, when they had next to nothing."

"So he brings all his girlfriends in here?" And suddenly I'm feeling small, crushing the growing hope that the fantasy in my head of a future with Miles in it just might work out.

"No, he's never brought a woman here," Sonia says, shaking her head. "Which goes to show the types of women he's used to dating."

She ushers me into a dressing room and I'm still hung up on her last comment. Does she mean that his ex-girlfriends or dates were high-maintenance and didn't shop here? Or is she going to turn me into a miniature version of his mother?

I've only seen a couple images of his mom, and she has a lot of the same light features he does, along with the light brown eyes.

I try on what feels like a million different styles of bra. The ones we settle on actually make a difference, and I can tell now why having someone measure the girls is better than playing roulette with the ones on the racks.

I've never shopped this long and I think I submitted all decisions to Sonia half-way through. By the end of at least four hours, I think we've covered everything from shoes to accessories to formal wear. My brain is mush after giving my opinion on every piece tried on.

"Hey," Miles says, walking up next to me and resting his hand on my lower back again. Warning sirens go off in my brain, but I can't break away from his touch. Who knew that something like this could make my legs all gooey?

The only touching with Clay or Cameron was the obligatory hug and then the making out. But after the cheek kiss earlier, I'm beginning to think they had no idea what they were doing. Because Miles blows all of that out of the water and our lips haven't even touched yet. Er, well, if they do because of rule three. Or was it two? My brain is fuzzy with him standing so close.

We're standing next to the register and Miles says, "Did you survive?"

I'm like a statue and Sonia smiles and nods. "She did great. Carl says he'll get your suits ready within the week, Mr. Clark, and I'll have them delivered to your loft. Dani, we'll work on tailoring a couple pairs of pants," she says, looking down at a notebook she'd written in throughout the day. "The silver formal gown will be ready by tomorrow, and the other three will be done before any further events."

"Awesome. I can't wait to see you in them," Miles says.

In a weird way, I'm kind of happy he didn't see the dresses I chose.

I know, I know. This is a fake relationship. I shouldn't care what his expression is like when he sees me for the first time. But I also didn't get that many chances for a first look. Clay had only taken me to prom our senior year after I begged to go to a dance ever since we began dating. Even when I came down our small staircase, he'd been too engrossed in a baseball game Landon had been watching to turn around and look at me.

Those red flags just keep lining up, in hindsight. That is number one hundred and five.

My breathing picks up and I might start hyperventilating. "Thank you, Sonia. I'm going to walk outside for a moment," I say to Miles. He nods, looking concerned.

"Are we good to go, Sonia?" I hear him say behind me.

"Yes, thank you, sir."

"Again, Sonia. You can just call me Miles."

It isn't too long before he's next to me, holding several smaller bags that I'd forgotten to take when my freak out started.

"Are you okay? What's wrong?" Miles asks. I can see him dip his head down to look at me, but I don't make eye contact.

"Do you think this will work? I mean, I've never been fitted for anything, let alone this much clothing. You've got to let me pay you back for this." I'd have to take out another job, or donate an insane amount of plasma, but it would be worth it for some of the clothing that had been piled up for me.

Miles chuckles next to me. "You're not going to pay me back. I can afford it, and I want to do it. You deserve it."

I raise an eyebrow. "I deserve it? Miles, you hardly know me."

He shrugs. "I've learned a lot about you in a short time, which is saying something. So enjoy it. And let's do something."

My stomach rumbles. "How about we cash in on that promise of pretzels and cheese?"

He laughs and nods. "I think we can handle that."

One step at a time, Dani.

We haven't even made it a week and I'm already panicking about this relationship. But maybe it's better than not caring, like I had toward the end of my relationship with Clay. And Cameron. Just go with it. That's my new motto.

I hope it doesn't mean I'll crash and burn by the end.

CHAPTER 15
Miles

I t's been a while since I've been nervous about a date. Hanging out with Dani and Oliver had been easy and I realize now it wasn't a true test of how we'd do at an actual event. Our first big outing as a couple has me hoping I'll be able to play the part.

Dani I don't worry about. It's me, constantly muddling things up. And being so close to her in the mall had my emotions heading into overdrive, which would be good if I hadn't started our relationship by asking her to be my fake girlfriend and then further cementing it by being happy about her calling us "friends."

I'm a mess.

And I nearly kissed her.

It's been less than a week with several to go and I'm worried I'll be the heartbroken one by the end of this arrangement. Stuck in the friend zone wouldn't be all that bad, but Dani is the first woman I've actually wanted to hang out with more than getting dinner and drinks.

"I don't think I'm ready for this," I say, glancing in the mirror. There's a reason I never joined any of the school plays or musicals. My acting abilities struggle.

"Yes, you are," Jack says, stopping by my loft. He's dressed in a tux and I'm still fumbling with the bow tie. Whoever invented it was bent on making a man crazy.

I walk into my bedroom again and work to straighten the mess around my collar.

"How are things going with your fake girlfriend?" Jack asks, settling into the sofa in the living room just outside my door.

"Good, really good."

"So, are you thinking about changing it to a real relationship?" Jack's voice is strangled, as if it's killing him to get the words out.

I sigh, pulling the loops of the tie and making sure it's in position. I walk out to grab the coat. "You haven't even met her. What makes you think that's the direction we're going?" I'm not sure what it was that set me off, probably the tie, but frustration grows like a web throughout my chest.

Jack shrugs and grins. "I haven't seen you this flustered in a while, bro." He glances down at my tie and I touch it again, making sure it hasn't moved. "I guess we'll see tonight, won't we?"

"See what?"

"If there's chemistry or not." Jack waggles his eyebrows and I shake my head.

"It's possible anything will be one-sided no matter how long the fake part of our relationship exists."

With a frown, Jack says, "Why do you say that?"

I swallow, trying to pull the shame down with it. "Dani says we're friends. I think I'm stuck in the friend zone."

"But you want more?" Jack's eyes are narrowed on my face, a sign he's mentally recording this conversation to throw back at me later. His memory is just that good.

"Again, I mean, things are really good. I haven't been able to talk to a woman like this in my entire dating history. Is that because we don't have the pressure of a relationship weighing us down? Or is it just the women I've dated?"

"Maybe it's just the magic of Dani Higgins?" Jack laughs. "You don't usually get this worked up about a woman, Miles. It suits you."

I sink into the other side of the couch and groan. "The things we do to avoid irritating situations." If only I'd just left things alone, maybe I'd be a happy bachelor instead of in a limbo-like pretend relationship.

"What? Create better ones?" We both laugh at that and the old grandfather clock in the corner chimes that it's time to go get our dates.

"Are you ready, Grandfather Time?" Jack asks, slapping me on the back.

"I'm just glad you'll be suffering there next to me." I grab my phone and wallet, locking the door once we're outside. "Who's your date of the night?"

Jack takes several slow steps. I have to slow down so he won't keep teasing me about wanting to see Dani.

"Diane. The one from Christmas last year? I figured I'd give her another chance."

"Maybe you should try that app, you know, the Love, Austen one," I say with a grin. "Since you decided to torpedo my account."

He shakes his head, frowning. "Whatever. I was trying to be you. All uptight and irritated when it comes to women." He pauses a moment and says, "Then again, having Dani around you has helped a lot. You're definitely not as defensive as before."

We get into the limo parked against the curb outside and give the driver directions to Diane's place.

"I'll take that as a compliment."

"You should." His gaze gets a far-off look and I wonder what about this situation has him so somber. The man is usually all about the jokes.

"What's bugging you tonight?" I ask, settling into the seat next to one of the doors.

Jack shakes his head. "Typical stuff. My parents are threatening to cut me off if I don't 'get my act together'." He says the last few words in a high-pitched tone, trying to imitate his mother.

I laugh and nod. "Maybe we should move to another country and become hermits."

"Nah," Jack says. "I need people to live. They're my best source of entertainment."

We pick up Diane and I want to strangle her within the first five minutes on the drive to Dani's house. Okay, strangle is a little aggressive, but the high-pitched, nasally voice grates on my nerves and makes me want to jump out the window. Think Janice from *Friends*.

"Who are we picking up in this neighborhood?" Diane asks, disgust written all over her face.

"My date," I say, smiling.

The driver stops outside the house with the yellow door and instead of flamingos all over the yard this time, there are mounds of clipped grass and twigs heaped up.

"They must have some strange neighbors," I mutter. I knock on the door, trying to breathe out the nerves charging through me.

The door opens and three sets of eyes stare back at me. It's like they're fighting for the spot.

"Hey, uh, is Dani here?" And ready? It had been fun to talk to Dani's roommates the other day, but right now, I just want to get her and start the night.

"Right here," Dani says, and I think I see a hand waving behind the mini-mob. They part for her and I see her in an elegant deep blue dress we'd bought at the department store on our trip. It fits her well, showing off her curves and extending all the way to the floor. But it's the light application of a dark pink lipstick that draws me in, making me want to cover them with my own.

I shake my head, knowing I shouldn't be thinking about that at all, at least not right now. Turning my gaze to focus on her movements as she's putting in an earring, doesn't help much, as the color of the dress accentuates her eyes.

"Wow, you look amazing." I step inside and almost forget we've got an audience. If those feelings of attraction had been undecided about Dani before tonight, this sends them over the edge. My crush on my fake girlfriend is on the rise.

Dani looks at me with a quick smile and I see a hint of nerves in her expression. "Thank you. You look hot." Her eyes nearly dance as she grins at me.

Is she saying that because it's true for her? Or is that part of the display for her roomies?

She turns to Evie and says, "Did I forget anything?"

Evie steps forward with a clutch that matches the dress, the rim of it encrusted in gems. "Now you're ready for the ball, Princess Dani."

The roommates chuckle, but I'm doing everything I can to hold back stepping up to her and kissing her senseless.

Must. Stay. Still.

I hold out my arm for her, and we walk out to the limo. Her roommates continue to chirp behind us, but I'm too wrapped up in her to think about anything else. The wind picks up, carrying with it a hint of perfume, and I like it.

"Do I look that different?" Dani asks, her long eyelashes fluttering a bit.

This is the most anxious I've seen her, and I want to reassure her everything is okay.

I shake my head. "No. You're always beautiful."

She rolls her eyes, not taking me seriously. "Thanks for that. Are we ready for the night?"

"We're about to find out."

I open the door for her, and she slides into the limo, blinking against the darkness. From the looks of Diane and Jack, we've interrupted a make-out session. She's sitting back against the seat, wiping her lips and Jack leans forward, trying to look casual. There's a hint of color around his mouth, giving him away.

"I leave you two alone for a few minutes," I say, laughing as I shake my head.

"This must be Dani," Jack says. The perfect tactic to deflect attention.

"Yes," I say, pointing to Dani. "Dani, this is Jack and his date, Diane. Jack and Diane, this is Dani."

Dani is smiling wide now. "You two sound like you're straight out of an eighties song."

It takes a moment, but her words sink in and I laugh. "That's so true." I pull out my phone and look up the song by John Mellencamp, playing it for the other two to recognize.

"I've never heard that song," Diane says, looking confused.

I share a quick glance with Dani, surprised we can communicate a bit through a shared glance. We settle into the seat and in a quick motion, I reach over and sweep her hand into mine. Might as well "practice" now.

"So what is the event we're attending?" Dani asks, her face so close to me that my gaze lingers on her lips, wishing for a moment alone from our audience. Instead, I take a second to answer her question.

"It's a charity event put on by the local board of health. Most of the proceeds go toward the Children's Hospital."

She shifts closer, her entire left side flush against my right. "That's really cool," she says. "One of my sisters broke her arm when she was about five. They sent her to the Children's Hospital to get the cast. It's good to know that a fun party can help the kids."

Jack snorts. "I don't know if you want to call it fun just yet."

I glance over to see Dani's curious expression and say, "His mother is the party planner for most of the upper echelon parties. Jack has been to too many of these to care."

Dani turns to focus on Jack and I'm curious what she'll say about that. "So why keep attending?"

"Inheritance. My lovely little lifestyle would go poof." He

makes a motion to emphasize his words and while in some ways it's true, the way he's acting is off. Exaggerated and annoyed.

I'll have to ask him about it later, figure out how serious his parents are about cutting him off.

Once we make it to the venue, I help Dani out of the car but give Jack a quick frown, trying to tell him to chill and just enjoy the night. He will eventually, but it's the first three hours that are the hardest for him. With his mother inspecting everything at all times, he's happiest when leaving.

As long as I've got Dani by my side, I might make it out of this shark tank alive.

CHAPTER 16
Dani

To describe my reaction to this place as amazed would be an understatement. Hundreds of lights and bulbs hang around the room making it feel like we could be on a beach in Miami instead of an indoor event in Boston.

"Are these events all this fancy?" I whisper, enjoying the close proximity to Miles. He smells divine and it's hard to hear each other over the talking of so many people. And other reasons. I'm pretty sure my nerve endings where our bodies touched in the limo are fried.

Miles nods back and forth. "A lot of them. There are some featuring a theme. I've come to this one in a costume before."

That conjures up several options, almost like Miles is a paper doll and I'm rearranging outfits to get the right look. "What costume did you choose?"

"A doctor. My ex got it for me."

I raise an eyebrow, shaking my head. "You didn't even try to come up with something? Miles, it's okay to express yourself in personal things from time to time."

He stares at me, his expression way more serious than I'd meant it to be. "True. I'll have to keep that in mind."

We make our way through several groups of people, Miles

nodding and saying hello to many. Once we find a spot near the refreshments, I take a breath and give myself a mental pep talk.

"You've got this, Dani. These people are just people. Just be your cool self and keep going."

I could be charming and witty, but all I want right now is to be at home, vegging on the couch with a pint of ice cream in hand. It's possible the beauty of the room has turned to overstimulation.

"Ah, Miles," a man says, walking up to us. "It's good to see you here again. Hopefully the business is going well."

Miles gives the man his professional smile, which doesn't light up his face. "It is, thank you. We're hoping to get a few things ready for the hospitals this year. As always, if there's anything you need, we're here to help."

"A discount helps, son," the man says, chuckling.

With a nod, Miles says, "For sure. We're working on a tiered program to allow that to happen, depending on units ordered."

"I'll believe that when I see it." The man raises his glass and heads in another direction.

"Who was that?" I ask, grabbing onto Miles's arm.

"The head of Massachusetts General Hospital." The vein near his temple has popped out and a light shade of red blankets his face.

I examine every part of him, noticing how tense he's become. "Are you okay? I guess I don't understand everything that goes into your business, but I'd like to help." As his fake girlfriend, it's the least I can do.

Miles looks at me and his fury softens somewhat. "He's kind of a jerk. He likes to haggle, and my mom has never been one for negotiating prices."

"So his dig was at the fact she's still head of the company."

He nods. "That's how I took it."

"That seems to be the favorite angle for people to take against you. Okay, who else should we watch out for?" I ask, searching the crowd of unfamiliar faces.

Miles takes my hand, and we walk to one of the small tables. He scoots my chair in and scans the room. "There's too many, Dani. I'd be naming the whole place."

I take his face in my hands and turn him so he's facing me. He looks like he's about to have a panic attack.

"It's fine. Do what you usually do and I'll be your support system right here." I drop my hands and glance around the room once more. "We can have a code word, or a signal or something. I'm great at distractions and I'm wearing heels again, so we've got options."

He laughs. "How about ice cream?"

"I love it." A few seconds go by and I realize he's talking about the code word. I must be nervous. "As a code word, of course."

His lips twitch and his eyes stare into mine. "Thank you. You don't know how much I appreciate that offer."

"Has this happened to you before?" I ask, not really sure how to emphasize the "this" without giving it a name. The increased breathing and the fight or flight in his eyes. He's usually so calm and collected that what had looked like an anxiety attack surprises me.

He nods. "Every once in a while, the crowd seems overwhelming. But if I take a step back and breathe, I can usually survive the rest of the event."

"Do you know what triggers it?" I ask, adjusting a section of hair that fell out of my half-updo.

"Stress."

I wave my hands in front of him and ask, "Okay, Mr. Wordy. Let's talk this through."

He squints and gives me a half-smile. "You want to walk me through my stress? I'm pretty sure that will only make things worse."

"It's worth a try," I say with a shrug. "My youngest sister, Sami, used to have something similar when she would run for school officer, or try out for one of the teams. It helped her walk through what she was feeling, and we'd help her see that there was no life-altering consequence."

"Yeah, I could definitely use that right now."

"Hey you two," a voice says behind us. I glance up to see Diane and Jack walking toward us.

"Hey," Miles says, forcing a smile.

Jack takes a look at Miles and says, "That bad this time, huh?"

"I'll be fine. Maybe we should dance." The music starts again, and several people head out on the dance floor.

It's now my turn to panic. "Um...yeah. You see, I've got two left feet and I would hate to ruin your shiny shoes—" Miles takes my hand and pulls me up, cutting off my words.

"Well, then we'll walk through it together," he says, the first genuine smile appearing since we walked into the room.

I take in a deep breath, hoping I won't make a complete fool out of myself. "We probably should have had a dancing lesson. Or twelve," I whisper into his ear.

"You'll be fine. Just follow my lead." He twists me around, holding my hand in his and then resting his other hand near my waist. "Back, sidestep, forward, sidestep."

I have to look down and mentally count out the steps, but at least I haven't tripped. Yet.

"Yeah, I've never done anything more than sway," I say, grinning at him.

"What's the sway?" Miles asks, flashing his straight white teeth.

"Both my hands are around your neck and both your arms are around my waist and we just sort of sway back and forth until the song is over."

Miles chuckles. "Yeah, that's not what we're doing here." He dips me, and for several seconds I wonder if he's going to lean in for a kiss. I'm hoping for it actually.

He lifts me and we go back to the steps for a few moments, me trying to catch my breath. "See, you've got this."

"Teaching your date how to dance?" I don't recognize the

voice, but Miles's face pales, as if a ghost is standing right behind us.

I turn, seeing the familiar face from all the pictures of Miles when Kenzie web stalked him. The long brown hair, the gorgeous dress and a look in her eye that makes me suck in a breath.

This must be the ex-girlfriend.

"Tanya," Miles says, nodding. Instead of letting go of me, he pulls me closer, allowing me to get another deep breath of his cologne.

"I seem to remember you doing the same thing for me when we started dating. How cute," she says. Her eyes lock onto Miles and I'm tempted to raise my hand up in front of his face to break the trance.

"Hi, I'm Dani," I say, twisting in his arms enough to stretch out my hand to her. She looks at it and then raises her gaze back to Miles.

She pinches her lips together and says, "Who's your rent-a-girl?"

Anger bubbles up inside me and I take a step to break away from Miles's arms. "I'm no rent—"

"She's my fiancé," Miles says, causing both of us to stop and look at him. He reaches over and takes my hand, squeezing it while still focused on Tanya.

The woman is stunned, her mouth open a bit and her eyes wide. "Fiancé?"

And just like that, I'm basically a bobblehead doll, my focus bouncing between the two of them. I mean, we've stepped up our game a whole other level with one simple title change.

"Yes," he says. He might be back to giving one-word answers, but his gaze is laser-focused.

Tanya glances down at my hand and I realize it's the only thing that gives us away. An empty ring finger.

"I don't see the ring," she says, triumphantly.

"It's getting re-sized," I blurt out, making this up as I go. That is a plausible explanation, right?

She sneers at me and turns back to him. "I'm surprised the papers haven't picked this up just yet. It's a little soon for you to propose, isn't it?"

Wow, what did he see in her in the first place? The woman is like a viper. Then again, I'm not the model citizen of relationships.

"Are you keeping tabs on your ex?" I ask, surprising even myself.

Tanya ignores me and says, "She's definitely different than your type."

"Things are different between me and Dani. It was the right time. And she's more focused on me rather than her career aspirations." As flattered as I would like to feel about that compliment, I cringe thinking that my negotiation for this whole fake relationship was to ask him to come to the mixer. Not like I'm up for a promotion or anything one way or the other, but the whole thing leaves a sour taste in my mouth.

When my mind comes back to the present, I'm not sure if I should be playing fiancée or bodyguard because the intensity increases in their voices. I won't be surprised if a fight breaks out. Well, Miles is a gentleman and wouldn't do something here. At least I hope he won't ruin anything that benefits sick kids.

Without another word, Tanya walks away, heading for the drink table.

It's then Miles seems to have woken up from his fury.

"Hey there, Tiger. Do you want to explain what just happened?" I'm trying to be serious, but my mouth betrays me with a smile. While intense, the conversation has been somewhat comical, to me anyway.

"I, uh, yeah. Sorry about that." He runs a hand through his hair and the strands bounce back into place perfectly. How does that happen? Magic hair?

I tug on his sleeve, heading for a small alcove where prying eyes can't see us. "Okay, since you decided to make us one step away from marriage in our fairytale relationship, we probably need to go over a few things. Like what happened between you and the model-esque woman who was just here."

The muscle along his jaw bounces a bit, his eyes turning into a storm. "We dated for a little less than three years. She left when a business opportunity came up."

The facts are working slowly through my brain. "Wait, was she a co-worker?"

His jaw tightens and he nods. "I was over the team of researchers, and she was one of them. She rose in the ranks while we dated and then left once she'd received the 'experience' she needed for her real dream job."

"Awesome," I say, more peeved than anything. Nothing like using a good man to get what she wanted. I have to push back the guilt that fills me with that thought. Miles agreed to come to the mixer. It's not like I asked him to donate millions of dollars. "So what is her interest in you now? Why approach you?"

I'm leaning against the wall, and Miles leans next to me with one arm stretched higher to hold him up as he thinks about my question.

"Jealousy. She has a fear of missing out and seeing me happy is probably making her crazy." Miles shifts his gaze from my eyes down to my lips and back up again. We're in the perfect section for a little kissing action, but I'm not entirely sure he's up for it. He asked for a farce after all.

I laugh. "Okay, so we've upped the ante to fiancés. We're going to have to come up with a story for the proposal."

Miles closes his eyes and groans. "I didn't even think about that. We'll need a ring too." Instead of smiling, he frowns, looking defeated.

"Hey, hey," I say, moving to look right into his eyes. "It's fine. I'm still here and we'll figure this out. It's just a bump in the road."

There's a scream and an audible gasp over by the staircase. At first, I don't react because I know a total of three people here, four if I count Miles's awful ex. But as the crowd parts just enough to see, Diane is on the floor, trying to help Jack up.

Blood drips down onto his white shirt and to the ground.

"Miles, it's Jack," I say, pointing.

He turns and jogs over to his friend. "What happened?" I hear him say as I work my way through the crowd. The majority of people here don't know me and move in after Miles passes by, blocking my path.

Miles reaches out a hand and helps Jack stand up. "I was just dancing along and we caught the stair."

From the look of Miles's expression, he's not buying that answer.

Diane's eyes are wide and she's near tears. "You saved me," she says, wrapping her arms around Jack.

"We might want to get him to a hospital or a doctor or something," I say, pointing to the gash on his forehead. Head wounds bleed more than others, but in a place like this, rumors could swerve toward him dying just for the drama of the story.

Most of the room has stopped, everyone staring in our direction.

"I'll get the car," Miles says, pulling out his phone. "Let's head out to the street."

It seems like we're weaving through millions of people at this point, but as we pass one of the refreshment tables, I grab a stack of small paper napkins and hand them to Jack.

"Use this before you make the blood trail worse."

He accepts and presses them to his forehead. "I've been through worse. I'll be fine."

We walk out into the humid summer air and I'm grateful to see the limo pull up a moment later.

The driver gets out and opens the door. "Where are we heading, sir?"

"The emergency room at Mass General."

Jack scoffs. "It's not an emergency. I've got the number to my mother's plastic surgeon. We could just call—" His words break off as he leans against the seat, passing out.

Diane lets out a cry and tears fall down her cheeks.

I breathe in, patting her back. "He'll be all right. We'll get him to the hospital and all stitched up."

Glancing down, I notice blood on the strange diamond bracelet. It has several sections of points that stand out from it, reminding me of a classier biker accessory.

"Did this hit his head?" I ask, pointing to it.

She pauses her tears for a moment before crying even louder at the sight of the blood. "I hurt him. How did I hurt him?"

Jack opens his eyes and frowns but closes them again once Diane turns toward him.

Miles shares a concerned look with me and I shake my head. Nothing like a little drama to add to my first event. More like a little drama with the addition of fiancé added to my name.

But there are some good things here.

1. I didn't fall and make a scene.
2. I know a little more about Miles's ex.
3. We left before I fell.

I only have like eight more events to attend with Miles. Let's just hope they don't all end with a trip to the hospital.

CHAPTER 17

Miles

How did the night get so messed up in such a short amount of time?

I watch as Dani works to comfort Diane, just like she did for me when we first got there. She didn't belittle me and tell me to get over it, that people were watching everything I did. She'd taken the time to talk me through it.

And then Tanya had to show up. What was I thinking in dating the woman in the first place? And what short circuit had caused me to call Dani my fiancé?

Probably the fact that Tanya had used me to get exactly what and who she wanted. And my mother is still falling for her crap. Rubbing it in and seeing the look on her face when I lied about an engagement was rather satisfying.

And yet that elation has worn off on our way to the hospital. Of all the bizarre things Jack has done, I didn't see this one coming. But why had he not admitted that Diane was the one who cut him with her razor blade-like bracelet? He doesn't have plans for a future with her, especially after this.

Dani sits next to me, just going along with the crazy train over here and I'll have to remember to thank her a million times over after our journey together is through.

The driver pulls up to the hospital emergency room and we all pile out of the limo.

"I'll call you when we need a ride back home," I say to him through the window. He nods and pulls out of the drive.

"You guys don't need to be here," Jack says, the napkins in his hand a bright red.

Dani steps up next to me and says, "We're not dumping you here and heading home." She glances up and her whole body stiffens.

I want to question her about it, but one look at the lobby and I know we're going to be here for a while.

Jack shakes his head and steps back toward the main door. "There's got to be an urgent care or something open, right?"

A lady holding an ice pack against her arm shakes her head. "Those places close at nine or ten in the evening."

"Can't I just wave some money around?" Jack slumps into a chair and closes his eyes as his head falls back against the wall.

"We were just at the party with some people from the hospital," Diane says, taking the seat next to Jack and stroking his arm up and down. "I'm sure you can find someone to talk to about that. Are you okay?" she yells while shaking him.

Jack jerks his arm away, irritation written all over his face.

I shake my head, scanning the room. There are several other patients with varying degrees of outward injury. The ones I can't see probably have something else they're in need of because why sit for hours in the hospital when nothing is wrong? "Waving money won't help us."

Diane is still in hysterics and while I'm not sure what to do, Dani pulls the woman to her, and they walk in the direction of the restrooms.

"What really happened?" I ask Jack as I sit down next to him.

Jack shakes his head. "Diane was drinking her wine while we talked to those investment guys and their wives. And you know her, she tends to talk with her hands."

"She really sliced you with her bracelet?" I say, glancing over at him.

Jack nods. "Yep, that she did. This might be the last time we go out."

"That's what you said the last time," I say, chuckling.

This is not where I thought we'd end up tonight.

Dani and Diane walk back and sit down next to me. Diane's head leans on her shoulder as a wave of sobs wracks her body.

"Are you all right?" I say, turning to Dani.

"Yeah," she says, blowing out a breath as she glances around.

She's wearing the same tight expression she had before, when she'd walked out of Bergdorf's at the mall.

I reach over and take her hand in mine, drawing little circles on the back with my thumb.

"Really?" I press.

She gives me a small smile and says, "Hospitals aren't my favorite place in the world."

"I get that," I say, leaning back against the wall. "Why?"

"We spent a lot of time here when my dad was sick. I can still remember toward the end that he smelled just like this. Antiseptic and sterile."

My heart reaches out for her, and I'm surprised by how much I wish I could protect her from the onslaught of feelings. But then again, I start to think of the short amount of time I was here with my dad.

"That's hard. I'm sorry. Do you want me to call a cab to take you home?"

She shakes her head, bobbing Diane's head a couple times with the action. "No, I'll be fine. Let's get Jack stitched up and we'll all head back together."

I watch as she leans her head back and closes her eyes. The woman next to me couldn't be more different than my ex. Kind, funny, spunky. Real.

She hasn't played games to get me to comply with her requests, hasn't tried to negotiate some elaborate ruse to get what she wants. Dani is just herself, unapologetically, and it's refreshing.

Without opening her eyes, she says, "At some point we need to talk about the fiancé situation."

I laugh out loud and nod, attracting the attention of several other people in the waiting room. "We will definitely do that. Just tell me you don't need to renegotiate the contract."

She shakes her head, her eyes popping open as the grin crosses her face. "No, I still owe you way more than I can afford at the moment."

I squeeze her hand, grateful to have her by my side. Without the hysterics.

But how long will this last without a contract?

CHAPTER 18

Dani

S leep is the only thing I want to think about right now. After a long night in the ER, I don't want to do much of anything.

We had to sit for at least two hours before Jack was seen by a doctor and then another two before he was finally released.

The part of the event we'd been to had been fun. Okay, I don't know if I'd term it fun. Interesting is a better explanation.

Nothing like meeting my fake boyfr—I mean, fiancé's ex-girlfriend in a crowded room. At an event I'd been nervous about anyway. And then he'd changed out the status of our relationship as though she'd thrown down the challenge gauntlet to get him back.

I need to ask him about her, about their entire relationship and dynamic so I can be ready for next time. Because if anything, we'll probably be running into her again. It was just late last night, and my mind was stuck on the fact we were in a hospital. That made it hard to think straight and have any conversations at all.

My bedroom door opens, and I turn to see Kenzie and Evie standing there, looking curious.

"What do you want?" I groan, knowing I won't be able to go back to sleep anytime soon. It's Sunday morning and I need to recuperate after last night's drama fest before I start work again tomorrow.

"How was your night?" Kenzie asks, walking in and sitting on the side of my bed.

I sit up, pulling the covers up around my shoulders to keep the warmth. "Eventful."

"Like fiancé status eventful?" Kenzie asks, and my gaze bounces back and forth between her and Evie.

"What do you mean?" Glancing at my clock on the wall, it says it's only eight thirty, way too early to be up right now. "Why are you both awake?"

"Millie got up to head to work and saw something we thought would be interesting. She didn't want to wake you since you didn't get in until late," Kenzie says, leaning closer.

It's then I notice the tablet in Evie's hands. "Um, we figured you hadn't seen this."

She clicks the button on the tablet and there is a picture of Miles and me standing near the refreshment table. I hadn't even noticed someone taking pictures.

The headline is what draws my attention next, and I have to suck in a breath.

HEALTHCARE HEIR ENGAGED?

How did people know about that? We'd only been talking to one person. My stomach drops.

Tanya must have spread the word.

Why would she care enough about a new relationship for Miles, unless she still has feelings for him?

I usually steer clear of drama that involves me. The cruise with Landon and Rachelle had been fun because of the prodding and pushing I could do for my brother, while not having to be right in the middle of it.

But this is bordering on war territory and I'm not too excited about it.

Then I think of the man in the middle, the kind, caring, sweet Miles and how he's been able to change my jaded view of men in the past week. There might not be too many men like him out there, and I'm suddenly hoping that August never comes.

"So?" Kenzie asks, pointing to the tablet.

"So what? His jealous ex-girlfriend probably spread the news."

Evie leans closer, touching my shoulder in order to turn me enough to see my face. "Wait, you're not surprised by the fiancé rumors? Did he propose last night?"

I rub my face with my hands, trying to allow my mind to wake up enough for this conversation. This is why I didn't want to get up yet. My brain is lagging from the late night.

"We've talked about getting engaged," I say. I grimace because it's still the truth, but there are some serious omissions going on here.

Evie frowns and Kenzie looks like she's just as invested in the story. Didn't she forget I told her this was all fake?

"So the tabloids jumped the gun?" Evie uses her finger to scroll up the page and stops for a moment. "Wait, you've been dating for all of how long?"

Oh boy.

Think fast, Dani.

"Not very long. But there are couples out there who know they're going to marry each other after one date." I glance to Kenzie for help, but she avoids my stare and checks her phone.

"Dang, I've got to run to pick up that job application. I'll bring back donuts." She sprints to the door four steps away and leaves me with Evie's glare boring into my soul. I don't have anything nearby to throw at her either.

Evie leans forward and squeezes my hand in hers. "I know it's hard, Dani, but you don't have to marry the first guy who proposes to you. You were in a long relationship. I'm not saying you have to wait another five years with a guy before getting married, but surely ten days isn't quite enough time to figure it all out either."

The disbelief on her face is enough to pull a laugh from me, but I do my best to muffle it as a throat clearing moment.

And this is an interesting turn of events. "Do you have experience in this? Being proposed to?"

The thought of seeing Miles down on one knee asking me to be his wife might be too much. In what world could that happen, first of all, and secondly, if he went all out to create a story for us to tell, it would be a lot harder to think of it as fake.

Evie nodded. "I've had a few guys propose. Mostly drunk guys on a Friday night, but there was one who I considered."

I'm blinking rapidly, riveted on the story I'm hoping she'll continue. "And what happened?"

Of all the roommates, Evie is the only one who hasn't had a gentleman caller, as she would say, since I moved in.

"It didn't work out. He was a great guy, but I just didn't feel that spark, you know?"

A spark. Is that what I've been experiencing every time I'm around Miles? Or is that just a rush of hormones and the fact that a handsome guy is paying attention to me?

How has he turned my life upside down in such a short time?

"Be careful," Evie says. "I know things were hard when Clay broke up with you, but make sure to be honest with yourself. No amount of money can change your attitude to true happiness."

I nod, pushing back that shred of worry. "Thank you, Evie. I'll be fine. I'm sure we'll have to correct a few things about us being engaged and we'll be good to keep on like before. I mean, this happens to celebrities all the time, right?" Why do I feel like a deflated balloon when I say that? "He's coming to the mixer to help next weekend and then Sharon will finally be off my back, which will help us have more time to figure all this out."

Evie raises an eyebrow. "Are you sure about that? I mean, the woman has been on you from day one. She wasn't even excited when you told her one of the multi-billionaire alumni had accepted your request to attend the mixer."

"She was a little excited," I say. Why am I defending her?

"Not enough to stop you from calling others." Evie sits back, leaning on her hands. "Maybe Miles can help you with that."

"With what?"

"With getting people to your mixer. He knows a ton of people and he might be able to pull some guys out of the woodwork for you."

I nod, tapping my pointer finger to my lips. "That's a great idea. I'll have to see what I can do."

My mind wonders if his group of friends were some he'd gone to college with. And what was the rule about inviting people who weren't alumni to the mixer?

I'd have to figure that out once I got going this morning.

"Okay, I'm awake. Anyone start the coffee?" I slip out of my bed and head toward the door.

"Millie did before she headed out for work."

I raise an eyebrow. "I swear her employers never let her have a weekend free."

Evie shakes her head. "I'm usually anti-confrontation, but I wonder if she can break her contract. There have to be a bunch of families here who need nannies. And she's a good one."

"We'll have to find some time and go out to dinner or a movie with her. Give her a taste of what Boston is really like." Millie had come from the South, planning to work for the year and then figure out the direction she wants to go in life after. But at this rate, she'd go home thinking Boston equals work.

Evie grabs ingredients to make pancakes and I start the coffee maker with a new pot, since the other one is almost dry.

My phone buzzes in the pocket of my hoodie. I pull it out and stare at the message, allowing myself a grin. Okay, I'm a sucker for anything that gives me butterflies and Miles seems to be the butterfly keeper.

Miles: How are you this morning?

Joy fills me, followed by an ache that this could never be my real life. I'd been fine, thinking that I'm with Miles in a support capacity only. But my heart is inching toward the cliff of true love, something it's never experienced before. Clay never made me feel like this.

Just my luck, the only guy who wants me at his side is the one who asks for a fake relationship. Heartbreak is in my future. I don't read crystal balls, but from the rollercoaster of emotions shooting through me this morning, it's inevitable.

CHAPTER 19
Miles

I've refreshed my screen at least three times since I sent the text message. I know, ridiculous that I'm wondering what Dani is up to this early on a Sunday morning, but the message says read with the time stamp next to it.

The three little dots pop up and then disappear. Start, stop. This happens at least three more times before a message comes through.

Dani: Good.

That's it? I need to calm down. After all that happened last night, there's a connection between us. Maybe she doesn't feel it, but the invisible thread gets shorter every time I'm with her.

Dani: Sorry. Waiting on coffee.

I smile, relaxing into my chair. Since when did I become so caught up in the hidden meanings behind a text? I type out a few words, wanting to keep the conversation going while she wakes up.

Me: Jack is still alive. I think the doctor did a great job considering who he was working with.

Nothing for several seconds and I make myself get up and walk around. I probably need some food too. It's the first morning I haven't worked out in a while and my whole routine is thrown off.

Dani: That's what he gets when his date is a wannabe ninja.

I spray the sip of coffee in my mouth all over the counter. That's a good way to describe Diane's attire from the night before.

Me: What are your plans for today?

Am I fishing? I might be fishing a bit. I don't have a meeting or a lunch to attend today, and doing something with Dani usually makes even the most boring thing, like shopping, more exciting.

Dani: Just a minute. Phone call with my mom.

I put the phone face down and head over to my room, needing a shower since I still smell like hospital. It had been almost one in the morning when I'd dropped off Dani at her house, meaning it was closer to one-thirty when I made it home, dead tired.

Stepping out of the shower, I'm not sure what to wear. I've had to wear business attire or suits for almost the last year straight. Some of the casual clothes Sonia recommended in my winter haul still have the tags on them. But it's too hot for any of those.

Instead, I walk out and check my phone. Two missed calls from my mom and another from Dani.

It's too early to deal with my mother. She'll have something to say about the reports of my engagement. Thanks a lot, Tanya.

So instead, I dial Dani's number and walk back into my room, sitting on the edge of my bed with a towel still around my waist.

"You're aliiiive!" Dani says when she answers.

I laugh and say, "Um, yes, yes I am."

"Sorry, it's from that one Frankenstein movie and it randomly popped into my head. How goes it?"

"Slow, but it's the weekend, right?"

She giggles and says, "For sure. Um, so, our friend Tanya

apparently spilled the beans about the nature of our relationship—"

"Are you writing a term paper on this?" I say, laughing harder.

"You gotta do what you gotta do. Have you written a twenty-five page paper? That's all about filler words. And if I feel the need to die in another couple years of school, I'll let you know."

"School does not equal death."

"Yes, it does. Anyway, because of the help of social media, my mother now thinks we're engaged. And she's madder than a kid hitting a hornet that I haven't introduced you."

I blow out a breath. "Isn't the phrase usually madder than a hornet?" It takes some effort to not full out laugh from the mistake.

"Yes, unless you're my younger sister who doesn't fear things that can sting."

"She hasn't disowned you or anything, right? Your mom, I mean." From everything I've heard about the Higgins family, it consists of everything mine never has. Getting her in trouble with them is not something I want to jeopardize with the current pretend nature of our relationship.

"Not exactly, no. But she's called an emergency family game night tonight and I'll be kicked out of the family if we don't attend."

"Oh, so I'm supposed to attend, huh?" I'm baiting her to see what she'll say.

She clears her throat and it sounds like she's trying to mask a laugh. "I thought that was implied. So? Are you up for a ridiculous spread of potluck food and hours of games?"

I grin, trying to picture the rest of Dani's family. If they're all like her, it will be an evening of fun and laughter.

"I think I can manage that. What time should I pick you up?"

"She wants to start around two. So one-thirty? Or I can come get you." Her voice sounds hesitant with those words.

I shake my head and say, "Game night that starts in the afternoon?"

"Yep, yeah, we're crazy like that, Miles," she says, and I love the way my name sounds when she says it.

"Okay, I'll be there just before one-thirty." I pause a moment, glancing into my closet one more time. "Hey Dani, what's the dress code for family game night?"

It sounds like a lame question, but I've never taken part in something like this.

"Casual. And not business casual either. Pajama pants, sweats, t-shirts. All are acceptable."

"Done. I'll see you then."

I stand to try and find the most random attire possible, settling on gray sweats and a navy-blue t-shirt. Standing in front of the mirror, I look boring compared to the taco pajama pants Dani wore the other day, but I'd have to work with this.

I don't know how she does it, but I'm more excited to hang out on a Sunday afternoon with Dani than dress up and hit the country club like I'm used to.

One more notch in the like charts for Dani. It's getting a lot harder to keep my feelings for this relationship on the fake side.

CHAPTER 20

Miles

I get stuck in traffic on my way to her house and Dani is already sitting outside on the porch. When she sees me approach, she picks up a pan next to her and walks up to the car, dressed in a flamingo print onesie.

She almost doesn't wait for me to come around and open the door, but she's carrying a pan with hot pads, which means she can't do it by herself anyway.

"What do you have there?" I ask, pointing to the tin foil covered pan.

"Zucchini cake," she says, slipping into the passenger seat and buckling her seat belt.

I wait until I climb back in to say, "What's that?" All I can picture are sliced zucchinis mashed up together inside a cake mix. Not appetizing.

She lifts the lid to reveal what looks like a normal chocolate cake, but with extra chocolate chips on top. "It's more sugar than veggies, but I figured I should use up one of the items I bought at the store last week when healthy me went grocery shopping."

Her grin causes me to laugh and a burst of joy shoots through me. I've never thought of laughter as being an important part of a relationship, but Dani makes it seem like a necessity.

"Healthy you?" I say, pulling away from the curb and following to the right where she's pointing. "Are you saying you have multiple personalities?"

Dani shakes her head. "No, not that I know of at least." She gives me a mischievous smile before continuing. "I was determined to eat better last week and so I bought a whole bunch of fruits and vegetables, avoiding the Oreo aisle altogether. It's been a rough week."

"That cake looks almost like an Oreo."

"Close enough. The cooked brown sugar on top is the best part of the whole thing."

She points toward one of the back roads instead of having me go up to a main road, like I'd planned.

"I guess we haven't ventured into the cooking skill conversation yet, have we?" I say, picking up speed to pass a car going ten under the speed limit.

She coughs and I turn to see if she's okay. "We kind of talked about it at dinner with Oliver. I'm like mediocre baker level. I might even qualify for that one show where all the cooks are awful."

"I'm about the same. I know a few recipes my grandma taught me back when she would watch me after school, but that's about it."

"Is she still alive?" Dani asks, giving me that expression that's so full of curiosity a guy could get hooked on trying to pique her interest all the time. "Your grandma, I mean?"

I shake my head. "She passed away about a year before my dad. That was a rough time. All the transitions and my mom used her grief as a force to become a workaholic."

The corner of Dani's mouth turns up a bit and she says, "And you've avoided doing that?"

As I mull over her question, I think back to the weeks before we started fake dating. I would usually work until at least seven every night, if not later, and now I'm barely dragging myself to the five o'clock hour.

"I don't think I could do that forever. There's so much to do in the world and chained to my desk isn't all that appealing."

"Are you ready for the mixer next Saturday? Maybe you'll make some contacts with people who could use your expertise. And it could be another outlet for you."

I glare over at her, making sure she knows I'm teasing. "Are you trying to turn me into a workaholic?"

Dani laughs, the sound full of joy. "No. I'm mostly just hoping to keep my own job. Jack didn't by chance go to Boston University with you, did he?"

The fact that she's asking about Jack has a stab of jealousy running through me. She didn't seem interested in him the night before. Then again, she's allowed to date whoever she wants after this is over. I'm just hoping he's not one of my best friends.

"Yeah, why?"

She sighs and leans her head back against the headrest. "Because my boss is driving me crazy about inviting more people to the event. Do you think he'd come?"

"I'm sure if you asked him, he'd consider it."

The frown on her face says volumes. "Why would it make any difference if I ask?"

So, she might not be into one of my best friends. That's encouraging. "Because I've already filled my current allowance of favors, and you have a clean slate."

"Is he really that bad?" she asks.

I shake my head and say, "No, Jack has just been through a lot over the years. He's one of those people who adds an extra level of sarcasm to everything."

It doesn't take much longer before we arrive.

"Here it is. Home, sweet home."

"This is where you grew up?" I ask after opening her door.

She shakes her head and says, "No, we sold our other house a few months after my father passed away. With all the bills piling up, it worked out to buy a smaller home for my mom."

It's interesting to see the other side of healthcare. My father had a heart attack and was gone in minutes, meaning he wasn't stuck in a hospital bed for months. And even if he was, we had the money to pay for the best of everything.

But hearing Dani's side of the story makes me realize just how important and expensive life-saving procedures can be. It renews my purpose in the family company, that we shouldn't be all about making money, but doing what we can to help those in a situation similar to the Higgins family.

"What did your dad pass away from?" I ask, right at the bottom stair to the porch.

"He had colon cancer. He didn't go in for scans in time to get it taken care of early." She gives me a small smile and I wish we were somewhere else. Somewhere we could talk a bit more about it. It's the most somber I've seen her since we met and as strong as she is, I'm sure there is still a lot of hurt underneath.

The front door opens before we have a chance to knock and a guy walks out, looking a lot like Dani.

"Dani, you made it. You better hurry in there. Mom's been cooking since this morning." The man looks over at me and says, "Hey, I'm Landon, Dani's older brother."

He sticks out his hand and does that thing where guys squeeze extra hard as a warning to not cause trouble.

I smile at him and nod. And then I squeeze a little harder until he pulls back. It's possible I don't see it right, but I think he flexes his fingers.

"Be nice, boys," Dani says, stepping through the front door. The space is small but tidy. There is an explosion of flowered wallpaper in different types throughout the living room and into the kitchen, making it almost feel like a field of blooms.

And by the look of the food piled up in platters along the island, Dani's brother is right.

"Hey Mom, where can I put this?"

"Dessert, appetizer, or rolls?" A plump woman with shorter light brown hair asks.

"Dessert," Dani says.

"Okay, we're putting those over on the far countertop." She's stirring something and the room smells amazing. "Once you've put it down, make sure to come over here and give me a hug."

Dani does as she's asked, looking like she's excited for this moment as she embraces her mother. My throat constricts a bit as I think about the last time my mother and I embraced. Probably elementary school.

The two step back and Dani says, "Mom, this is Miles Clark. Miles, this is my mom, Andrea Higgins."

Her mother scowls and says, "What? You don't even introduce him as your fiancé?"

"I, uh, well, I'm getting used to that," she says, looking at me with wide eyes. I'm not sure what to say to help her out of this.

Her mother takes Dani's left hand in hers and I remember the small box in my pocket. As discreetly as possible, I push the lid of the box up, pulling out the ring into my palm.

Her mother continues. "And where's your ring? I expected to see something about it in the articles Harper read to me earlier today, but there was nothing."

"Oh Mom, it's fine. We were waiting to tell you about the whole thing until—"

"Until we got the ring resized," I say. "I almost forgot to tell you that I picked it up yesterday before the jeweler's closed." I grimace at that explanation, because yesterday we hadn't been engaged at the time any real jewelers were open. I also picked it up from a drawer in my room and not an official jewelry store.

This is the ring I'd inherited from my grandmother. With everything that had happened at the last event, I figured this would be the easiest direction to go since our engagement wasn't planned. And for some reason, it felt right to have Dani wearing it. Maybe our relationship wouldn't last forever, but for now, it's like having Grandma Clark here with me.

Dani's eyes are wider than I've ever seen, and she's doing her best to act casual. "I didn't know, sweetheart."

That word on her lips has my heart racing as I take her hand from her mom and slip the ring onto the correct finger, relishing in the feel of her hand in mine. The ring is a tad loose, but passable for its purpose.

Her mother takes the hand back and leans over, oohing and aahing over the ring. I might be trying to avoid Dani's gaze because there are so many things we can't say here and now.

"What's going on in here?" a voice asks from behind us. I turn to see what looks to be a miniature of Dani.

"Harper, we're checking out Dani's engagement ring," Mrs. Higgins says, lifting Dani's hand with a twist.

"I'd love to be able to use my hand after tonight," Dani says, her eyes wide.

The young woman steps forward with disbelief written all over her face. "You're really engaged then? I thought you'd get back with Clay. Looks like I lost the bet."

"Thanks for the vote of confidence, sis," Dani says, wrinkling her nose in disgust.

"I'm Miles Clark." I step forward, with my hand outstretched for her to shake but she doesn't see it as she takes a seat at the counter.

Harper chews on a piece of gum loudly and nods. "Nice to meet you. You're the one willing to put up with our sister for life?"

"Harper," their mother crows. "Marriage isn't a life sentence."

She sits down and leans on the table. "For some it is."

"Where's Mal?" Dani asks, turning her focus to her mother.

"She should be here in a minute. We ran out of sugar and asked the neighbors if we could borrow some."

Running footsteps sound along the hallway and I turn to see who I assume is another sister of Dani's.

"Is dinner ready, Mom? I'm starving. I think I could eat a whole elephant right now."

I start to chuckle and the girl looks up at me. "Hey, new person. I'm Sami. Youngest but coolest of the Higgins siblings."

I laugh harder at that. This family doesn't lack for confidence. "Miles. Nice to meet you."

The door opens and in walk two other women, one of whom doesn't look like she is part of the family. It's been a long time since I've been in a room with so many women. And that was only for a business meeting.

"Ah, this must be the mystery man Dani is going to marry," the one on the left says. "I'm Mallory, second youngest in the family. And this is Rachelle, Landon's wifey."

"Ugh, why do you have to say it like that?" Harper says, twirling her gum around her pointer finger.

Dani rushes over and throws her arms around Rachelle's neck. "It's so good to see you. How was your honeymoon?"

The woman smiles and I feel like I'm in the dark with all this. We need a longer discussion about our families and our past to put all this together.

"It was so great. Perfect, even. We just got back this morning when we got the call. Apparently, Dani getting engaged is enough to hold two family game nights in one month." Rachelle smiles wide, but there's no malice in it. "I'm so excited for you." She leans forward and whispers something, to which Dani responds back.

Landon comes back in, walking over to stand next to me. "I have to say, man. Dani keeping a relationship quiet is kind of a big deal. How'd you do it?"

I pull at the collar of my t-shirt and say, "I'm just as surprised myself." Then, figuring I might as well get more information about the members of the family, I say, "Where did you two go on your honeymoon?"

And just like that, the hard exterior softens and Landon grins over at his wife. "We stayed at a resort on one of the islands where our ship stopped on the cruise. It had a lot of meaning, since it was our second attempt at getting married. I recommend it if you want a tropical honeymoon. And they have amazing room service." Landon winks and it takes me a second to understand what he means.

"That's great," I say, glancing over to make sure Dani isn't listening in. "You were engaged before?"

He nods, his smile falling a bit. "High school sweethearts, a month out from the wedding, and Rachelle's sister convinced me I would ruin Rachelle's life if we got married. We were apart a year before reuniting on the cruise."

Maybe that's why Dani's sister had thought Dani would get back together with her ex. "Congratulations on the nuptials. What line of work are you in?"

"Real estate."

Then everything starts to click as I remember Oliver talking with Dani at dinner. "I think I remember that. Roman is the owner of the company, correct?"

Landon's surprise makes me smile even more. "How'd you know that?"

"I'm good friends with one of his frat brothers from college. We made the connection when Dani was talking about the PopCandy earbuds you brought her from London."

There is pressure near my elbow, and I look down to see Dani's hands resting there and surprise on her face. "You remembered that?"

I shrug, not wanting to blurt out that I've carefully listened to everything she's mentioned in the past two weeks. Sure, I might've forgotten a few things, but I want to get to know her more, wondering if she's starting to feel the same way I am about our relationship.

"All right, everyone," Mama Higgins says. "We're so excited to have you all here tonight. We'll go ahead and begin with the food and then pull out the games."

The siblings line up at the island, pulling food onto plates before sitting down at the large oak table.

They laugh and chatter about different things, bringing up stories from childhood. The atmosphere in this house is completely different than where I grew up. My dad did the best he could to counteract my mother's mood swings and work obsessiveness, but there's something here that makes me feel like I'm home for the very first time.

And once I've got a taste of that, it's going to be hard to leave it. I shake my head, trying to get rid of the pessimistic thoughts. I'll let the doubts flood in later, after I've figured out the key to make my home feel like this.

CHAPTER 21
Dani

I'm not sure what I was thinking when I invited Miles over to my family game night. Maybe it was a temporary lack of judgment or that I wanted to spend more time with him.

The fact he remembers something so small from our conversation with Oliver at dinner the other night has my heart beating out of my chest.

And then my siblings have to crush that.

"Do you remember that one time Dani wanted to prank Randall next door and managed to steal all his underwear?" Harper says, trying to be the life of the party.

I frown, knowing I probably should've thought this through before bringing Miles into the fray. "It was one pair of underwear, and his brother gave it to us."

"You hung those on the line for a week to torture him," Harper says, mischief on her face.

Do I engage her with tales of her own? Instead, I try to bury that competitive edge and focus on eating the food. It's all so good.

We clean up and pull out the games. Miles looks a little confused and I remember I haven't explained anything to him.

"So, when we were little, we loved playing games. We could

never agree on the same game, so my parents came up with the number game to get us started. My mom comes up with a number and whoever gets the closest, we have to play their game first."

"Okay," he says, nodding.

I point to a closet that used to be used for extra blankets. It's the ultimate game storage now, since we've tried so many board games and card games over the past couple decades that the shelves are jam packed.

"Once my sisters are done picking their games, we'll pick our own."

Miles chuckles as we stand from our seats and walk over. "Wow, I didn't realize there were this many games on the market."

I laugh and say, "When we find a line of games we like, it's typical to buy all of them."

"What if I have no idea what they are or how to play?" Miles frowns, his gaze scanning the lines of boxes.

"That's okay," I say, touching his arm. I really need to stop making physical contact when not necessary, but the man is like a human magnet, pulling me closer all the time. Not like he knows that, but oh well. "What kinds of games do you like? That will help me narrow it down to a few options."

He glances at the games again and says, "I'm not sure I even know." There is a look of uncertainty and then his breathing picks up, a lot like at the party the night before.

I take his hands in mine and say, "Hey, look here." When he focuses those baby brown eyes on me, I have to use his hands as supports to not let my knees buckle all the way. "Breathe. It's okay. Even with all the blackmail stories my siblings like to tell, my family is a safe space."

He takes in a deep breath and nods. "Thank you."

Instead of bugging him again with something he's not ready for, I reach into the closet. "This is one of my favorite games right now."

"Skull King?" he says, his face softening back into a smile. "You have always wanted to be a pirate, huh?"

I give him fake surprise and say, "How did you know? Arrggh! We'll be together on this one." I reach out and take his hand, enjoying the fact that we're supposed to be playing up the nature of fiancés.

Once we settle into the table, our game is chosen to go third. We take turns explaining each game to him, except for the one Rachelle brought back from their honeymoon. None of us have heard of that one.

After the instructions are given for game number one, Miles reaches over and takes my hand under the table, intertwining our fingers. I'm pretty sure my insides start a rave. And is it weird that I never want it to end?

But the line is getting close, the one where if I cross it, I won't be able to return safely. I can either back off and keep my heart intact or keep going right over Heartbreak Hill. No Boston Marathon needed for that one.

We're there for over four hours, and we make it through everyone's game. Settlers of Cataan takes the longest and Miles seems to enjoy that one. Probably because we won from his strategical suggestion.

"How come you two haven't kissed at all?" Sami asks as we're cleaning up for the night. Landon and Rachelle have already taken off because of an early meeting he has to get to in the morning.

I blink a few times, trying to earn me some time before I answer. "What do you mean?"

"Landon and Rachelle have been kissing each other all night. What's your problem?" Harper says, her arms folded against her chest.

Here comes the panic Miles probably felt when asked to pick a game. My stomach ties itself into knots and I'm doing my best to focus on my sisters' faces.

"That's not always a sign of love," I say. Can I have those words back please?

Mallory leans against the counter. "Are you kidding? Kissing is the second sign of love."

"What's the first?" Sami asks, very interested in this conversation.

"Holding hands and hugging."

Sami nods. "Well, they've been holding hands all night."

Leave it to my sisters to analyze every movement. They'd probably make good reporters one day.

Harper turns back to me, her gaze bouncing between me and Miles. "I think they should kiss. I mean, you are engaged and everything."

Warning bells go off in my brain. Why do my sisters have to be so weird about stuff like this?

We'd talked about unnecessary PDA, and this seems to fit into the necessary category to keep up the act of our fake relationship. But what if he thinks I'm a bad kisser? Maybe that's why Clay and Cameron decided to move on with their lives.

I also had some of the delicious shrimp and cream cheese concoction my mother made, not thinking kissing was in my future. There's no acceptable way to smell my breath right here and now. And I'm in a flamingo onesie. Obviously, I didn't think this through.

My thoughts continue to spiral until Miles spins me around, placing a hand on the small of my back to pull me closer to him. He presses his lips to mine, and I go from rigid to completely relaxed.

Dang this guy can kiss! My brain is all fuzzy and the tingly sensation is all the way down to my toes. That sensation when you eat Pop rocks is basically how my lips feel, like I could spark a fire easily. I reach up, placing my hands on either side of his face and almost lose my balance as he deepens the kiss. He tastes sweet, like the chocolate cake I'd made. He'd tried it?

I catch a piece of hair near the nape of his neck and twirl it.

It's going to be hard not to want to kiss this man daily from here on out.

"Okay, okay," my mother says, bringing me back to reality. "I think that is a good enough display of your love for each other."

We break apart and laugh, but there's something in his eyes, like he's sorry to pull back?

I'm tempted to drag him out of here and find a secluded spot to continue our mini-make-out session.

But that's against the rules to our relationship.

We're loaded down with leftovers, and after saying goodbye to my family, Miles does his gentlemanly act and opens the car door for me.

We both sit back and sigh at the same time. This leads to laughing and I don't think I've ever been so happy.

"Thank you," Miles says. His eyes are soft and although he looks tired, his smile isn't.

"For what? Introducing you to the reason I'm so crazy?" I say, pointing toward the house.

He shakes his head. "You're not crazy. You just have a great relationship with your mom and siblings."

It's then I realize I still don't know much about his family. "Did you play many games growing up?"

He turns to start the car and I wonder if this conversation is over.

"I remember having Chutes and Ladders, but it was to help me learn to count as a young kid."

"You had a specific educational purpose for games?"

He smiles sadly. "Yeah, my mom was determined to get me into this fancy preschool and I had to pass a bunch of tests to be admitted."

From the slight panic moments I'd seen from him, I know he's under a lot of stress, but it makes me wonder how long he's been dealing with anxiety of certain situations.

"Thank you for being there for me. For not ripping me apart

when I freeze with a decision." He's focused on getting the car going and I wish I could take away some of his pain.

"Does that happen often for you?" I ask, watching as the muscles in his shoulders tighten a bit. There are good reasons for checking him out, I tell myself. Learning his body language, of course.

He shakes his head. "Not all the time, just when I'm faced with a lot of new decisions and don't have data for them."

"Like research?" It sounds odd to need that for everyday moments, like board games.

"My mom has always trained me to be prepared, to study people I might meet so I'll know what to talk about and how to act."

I don't know how to respond to that. "So in studying about something, you know you have a firm opinion about whatever the topic or discussion is."

He nods. "All I could think about when I looked into the game closet was all the information I didn't have to make an educated decision."

I reach over, taking his hand in mine and patting it with the other. "You don't ever need to worry about that with me."

Not that I could promise forever, but I'll be here as long as he wants me.

CHAPTER 22

Miles

Who am I? Here I am sharing my feelings and insecurities with Dani and I hardly recognize myself.

Everything I told her is true, that panic sets in every time I don't know the information to make a good decision. In our business, knowledge is power, because one misstep can cause the company hundreds of thousands of dollars, if not millions.

Talking to Dani about it makes me feel like a trained monkey who no longer has the trainer. Then again, I've felt like that ever since my father died. Not that he was an awful trainer, but he tried to give me as many of the tools to survive in the family business as possible. He'd been the one to play the games with me when I was small, and even though he told me that they were to help me with counting or different skills, I wonder now if that was just to keep my mother from getting mad that I wasn't constantly being quizzed on letters and numbers from flash cards.

I don't sleep much once I get home. Most of what I think about is that kiss with Dani.

The terrified look in her eyes when I turned her around in front of her mom and sisters that led to her almost melting in my arms. How the nerves in my lips acted as though they were on fire long after we pulled back.

I'm not sure why I reacted like I did, but kissing Dani is one of those experiences I don't need past research done for. My lips still tingle thinking about it as I walk into work the next morning.

Meeting her family and the banter they have among them is what makes their house into a home. I could tell they love each other by the way they care and support every person there, despite the endless teasing.

I'm in my office, sorting through emails when a knock comes at the door. I glance up to see my mother and remember the missed calls I never returned.

"Good morning, Mom."

"Miles, we have a lot to discuss." She steps inside and shuts the door. It's the first time I've ever seen her actually step inside my office. Usually I'm being summoned to hers.

She takes a seat on one of my uncomfortable chairs. Her eyes are narrowed and lips pinched tight. "What is this about you being engaged?"

I think back to giving my grandmother's ring to Dani and shame fills me. That's not a way to propose, even if it's supposed to be fake.

"Yes, Mom. To Dani Higgins."

"Didn't you just break up with the one who talked too much? What was her name? Lydia?"

"Amber. Yeah, we broke up a while ago." More like ten days ago.

"And so you're rushing into a relationship with a girl not even in any of our social circles? What if it doesn't work out?"

I shake my head. "Then I'll deal with it then. For now, I'm happy and excited. Something I haven't been in a long time."

"What about Tanya?" she asks.

"What about Tanya?" I mirror her posture, leaning forward so we can have this discussion now.

"Why won't you give her another chance? You two were inseparable for so long."

Frustration ebbs in my chest and I shake my head. "Because we've both changed, Mom."

I don't know why I try to protect Tanya, to make it seem like I'm the one who broke up with her in the first place, but I'm over all this. It's Monday morning and I need to get work done so I can go home and spend time with Dani. That's not something I ever thought I'd say, but I like it.

"Well, change is to be expected. Don't throw away your life for this girl."

"She's a woman, Mom. She's a college graduate and she's got a career. Don't keep downplaying that as though I'm dating a leech."

My mother snaps her mouth shut. "Well, you have dated some of those in the past year."

There's another knock on the door and my mother's assistant pokes her head into the room. "There's a call for you from the hospital board."

"Thank you, Chesney." She turns her focus toward me as she stands up. "We're not done with this conversation."

As far as I'm concerned, we are.

I'm falling for Dani, and while the thought scares me because she could stomp on my heart and leave me at any point, there's something so different about being with her compared to Tanya or any of the other women I've dated.

She makes me want to be better.

I know it's a cheesy sentiment, but if the person I'm with doesn't inspire change and a hope for the future, then what good is that going to do me?

CHAPTER 23

Dani

Welcome to the new week. Everything I've planned is starting to implode.

We're only six days out from the mixer and I get a call from Sharon on my way in that a pipe burst in the convention room where we'd been planning to do the mixer this coming weekend.

"We won't be able to use it at all," she says, her voice bordering on hysteria.

I'm not sure why she's worrying about it. The mixer is my bread and butter, what I'm going to have to prove and show to her and the upper bosses by the end of the summer in order to keep my job.

"Are there any other venues open for Saturday?" I ask, trying to do a mental walk through of the rest of the buildings on campus. There aren't too many that would be a good fit for the numbers we're hoping for.

"No, all of them are booked."

"Maybe I can look outside campus. There's got to be something open we can use on such short notice." After all the research I've done over the past couple weeks, what is one more search?

"That's not possible. We need people to come to campus and

feel nostalgic. To get them to open their wallets in order to donate to the school." Sharon's words are firm, to the point I have to wonder if she's okay.

Irritation clouds my vision and I don't think before I say, "Is money really all you care about?"

There is silence for several moments and I want to curl in a ball I feel so bad.

When Sharon speaks, her voice is soft but sharp. "The money donated to the school supports both your job and mine, as well as several others in the department. My child was just diagnosed with kidney failure, Danielle. So yeah, I might be obsessed with making this a success because a lot is riding on it."

I didn't think I could feel any smaller than I had a few moments ago and then she hits me with that.

"I'm so, so sorry, Sharon." I pause, taking in a deep breath before tears fall. "I had no idea. I just thought you hated me."

"No, the stress is getting to me. So while I appreciate you finding one guy who might be willing to donate to the school, we're going to need a few more to make it through budget cuts for the coming year."

Blowing out a breath, I wish I could go back and change my attitude at calling people a week ago.

I go through everything in my head, trying to find some solution as to how to fix this. "Did they say how long it will be until the damage can be fixed?"

Sharon hums for a moment and says, "I think they said it's mostly just drying things out. There might be patchwork on some of the lower walls, but it won't be dry by the weekend. And safety precautions make it so we can't have the event until everything is in working order."

I nod, looking at my calendar. "What if we move the event?"

"I just said we can't move it anywhere but the current place."

"Sorry, I mean, what if we move it out a couple weekends? Is there availability in, say, three weeks?" It would be getting close to the end of July, but changing the date might give us more time and I can work extra hard to get more people to show up.

Again there is silence on the other end of the phone. I wait, remembering patience is the best course of action right now.

"Okay, I just checked the website, and it looks like we could do it that last week of July. The problem is getting in touch with everyone about the change."

"Don't worry about that, Sharon. I'll take care of it. Do you mind if I work up some new invitations? We'll just email them out with the change so we don't waste more money on postage." I pause a moment and say, "I'll call all who've made a reservation already and let them know about the change as well."

"Good thinking. It's better to overcommunicate than not at all."

And that is something I need to remember in the future.

CHAPTER 24
Miles

M y phone buzzes and I smile when I see Dani's name next to a message.

Dani: You're off the hook this weekend.

Her text has me confused. I've checked my calendar and other emails but other than the mixer event I'd promised to attend, I don't have much else. And I know how much Dani is banking on me being there.

Instead of texting, I call, since I have a few minutes until my next meeting. After the conversation with my mother this morning, I'm in need of a cup of Dani's optimism.

"Hey, I got your text. What do you mean?"

She sighs and says, "The conference room we were going to have the mixer in had a pipe burst. We're moving the mixer to the last week in July. So if you know of anyone else who you can rope into coming that day, I'd appreciate it. What about Oliver? Did you go to college together?"

"No," I say, leaning back in my chair. I'd almost expected her to be in hysterics once she said the mixer is being delayed, but it sounds like she's already on top of a plan. "He went to Hawthorne University in California."

"Dang," she says. "Okay, well, give me Jack's—oh wait, I've

got him on this list here. The punk didn't answer me the first time."

I laugh at her irritation with my best friend and nod. "I can't wait to hear how that conversation goes."

"I'm a woman on a mission today." She pauses a moment and when she speaks again, her voice is softer. "Turns out my boss doesn't hate me. She's just going through a lot at home."

"I'm sorry. At least you found out what was going on."

Some papers rustle in the background and she says, "Yeah. Sorry, I didn't ask how you are. How's work going for you today?"

"Well, I had a conversation with my mother about you and how I could think of getting engaged this quickly. So our plan is working."

There is a sort of squeak from her, and I have to laugh. "Are you all right?"

"Good, great. Wonderful. Um, I wanted to ask you though, this ring is very unique and looks like it might be some kind of heirloom. Are you sure you want me toting it around on my finger?"

A mixture of worry and happiness flow through me. Happy because she's wearing the ring I gave her and worry because she sounds like she'd rather do anything but be engaged to me.

"Of course. I mean, it looks great on your hand."

"What I mean is, you didn't by chance purchase it at the store, did you?"

"No."

There's silence for a moment and she says, "That's what I was afraid of."

I rub the back of my neck, wishing I could see her face in person. "Afraid of what?"

"That this ring has special meaning to your family and I'll be wrecked if I lose it."

"Dani, you'll be fine. It fits well and it works for the purposes.

Although, I thought I'd have a moment to plan out a proposal so we'd have a story."

She laughs and says, "If you'd proposed in my mother's kitchen, there would've been an uproar and we still would be there. My mother's interrogation tactics are solid."

I laugh along with her. "I don't doubt it."

Several moments of silence pass between us and I speak again. "Since we're not busy with the mixer this weekend, do you want to go somewhere? A movie, maybe?"

Why does it feel odd to be asking her out even though we've been spending so much time together?

Probably because I want things to be real between us now. Of all the women I've dated, and there really haven't been *that* many I was interested in or wanted to spend more time with, and Dani falls into both. Tanya and I would take breaks from seeing each other for at least a week at a time. It seems like the more days pass, I can't imagine why I would need a break with Dani.

"I actually promised my roommate I'd stay in and watch the hockey game."

"Which hockey game?" In the city of Boston, there are a number of great hockey teams.

"NHL. Boston Breeze. She's kind of a crazy fan."

Grinning, I think through the options. "What if we make it an event and go to the game?"

Dani laughs. "Um, that would be great, but getting tickets to a playoff game this late would break my bank account."

"No need for that. It'll be my treat."

With a groan, Dani says, "You're not paying for my ticket to a hockey game. After all you've already paid for—"

"What if I don't pay for it but I know someone who can get us the tickets."

A healthy pause follows, and she finally says, "Well, then I wouldn't feel so bad."

I laugh, shaking my head at the idea. "Okay, would all your roommates like to join?"

"I'm not sure about Millie's schedule, but it could be a fun night out with the roommates. Let me know the details and where to meet you."

When I hang up the phone, I dial Eliza, our business manager. Because the only way Dani is going to let me off the hook is if she thinks I didn't buy them.

CHAPTER 25

Dani

I don't want to be "that" girl, but having connections like Miles does makes life a little more fun. Obviously we would've made the night memorable by hanging out to watch the Boston Breeze go against the Cincinnati Sabers at home, but there is something about sports in Boston.

Going to a Red Sox game is one of the ultimate highs in this city because the people love the game and love the team. The Boston Breeze is up there and gaining notoriety after several seasons with a strong lineup.

And Kenzie is practically freaking out every time I say anything about it.

Millie's boss said she could take the night off, which is great because the girl deserves a break.

And there's nothing better than a great playlist and everyone getting ready. It's been so long since I've had a girl's night out, okay, well I've never really had that. Clay was my weekend. And by the time I realized I missed out on some of the fun friend stuff, I didn't know where to turn.

And while I won't see Miles until the game, the pre-event getting ready has been a blast.

"Can you believe we're going to a playoff game for the

Breeze?" Kenzie screams. She's wearing a Breeze jersey with Carver on the back. She tied it near her waist so it accentuates her figure. Evie and I have chosen jeans and a comfy top. Millie opts for a skirt and t-shirt.

There are curling irons and brushes, cans of hairspray and hair protectant strewn all over the large bathroom counter. Makeup bags are open and we're just about ready. Millie turns on one of her favorite songs, dancing along to the music. It's fun to see a different side of her.

The doorbell rings.

"Who's that?" Evie asks, pausing before wrapping another section of hair around her curling iron.

I shake my head, putting the mascara wand back in the tube. "I'm not sure. I told Miles we'd meet him at the arena."

I go downstairs with quick steps, my curiosity gaining momentum with each movement. Opening the door, I note a man in a dark suit.

"Miss Dani Higgins?" he says, tipping his hat quickly. He's an older gentleman, with gray in his sideburns and his mustache, but his smile is bright. "Mr. Clark sent me over to escort you ladies to the game." I glance behind him to see a black limo.

"He did, did he?" I say, smiling at the idea. No matter the real status of our relationship, the man is good at thinking ahead and taking care of others. And here I am going from never riding in a limo to twice in one week.

"Thank you so much, uh, what's your name?" The most important piece of advice my father had ever shared with me was that learning people's names, no matter their situation or status, went a long way.

"Walter Fordham."

"Well, Walter. I'll tell my roommates to hurry up and we'll be out in a few minutes."

He nods and turns to walk back to the limo while I shut the door. Running up the stairs, I do a little dance.

"Are you having a seizure?" Kenzie asks.

Evie tries to hold back a laugh and says, "I think she's excited about something."

"Did your fiancé send you flowers?" Millie asks, turning as she holds up a brush for eye shadow.

"Better. He sent a limo to take us to the game."

Evie sighs. "That means we won't have to worry about the heat and the T."

Kenzie stands up and mimics my movements. "Are you sure the guy doesn't have siblings? A cousin who happens to be just like him, perhaps?"

The four of us take a few moments to laugh about that. "No, he's an only child."

Millie turns and says, "Wait, how did he react to going to family game night then?"

"I think he loved it. He told me he didn't play many games growing up." The memories of that night are tender, being able to help him calm down enough to enjoy it. And how can I forget the kiss? I think it's permanently burned into my brain at this point.

"I think we could all use our own Miles Clark," Evie says, turning back to her small mirror and applying eyeliner.

Sadness overtakes me as I glance around at my roommates. They're all fun, beautiful women with varying personalities, and they deserve—we deserve—to find someone who can complement that. Not that having a boyfriend or a husband is absolutely necessary to living a great life, but after watching Rachelle and Landon's life morph back into the near fairytale love story it was meant to be even after a break, I'd love to have that too someday.

Evie's admission about turning down a proposal and Kenzie's story of her ex proposing and then coming back for the ring, saying it was a mistake, makes my heart go out to them. But am I falling into that category?

I glance down at the ring on my finger, wondering what it will be like the day I have to give it back. It's beautiful, but I'd be okay with a string on my finger as long as Miles, or someone like him is in my life.

I hurry to change in my room, relishing in the quiet there. Even I could use a Miles Clark, one I can be with forever.

If only I hadn't agreed to play pretend in the first place.

CHAPTER 26
Dani

"Can we ask this guy if we can stop somewhere to get food along the way?" Millie whispers to me as we drive through the Boston streets.

"There should be food we can buy at the arena," Kenzie says, reapplying lip gloss.

The buzz of excitement in the limo is off the charts and I'm grateful for this chance to go out together and enjoy something that has been on Kenzie's lifetime bucket list.

Miles: Did the limo make it to you?

I grin as I see Miles's text and start tapping away.

Dani: He did and you've probably made all our dreams come true with tonight. Are you there already?

Miles: No. I might get there a few minutes late. I've just emailed you the tickets. They'll scan the code at the door and show you where to go.

Disappointment fills me and I hope he's not late because of work. He's already had a lot of conversations with his mother about our relationship and on the small chance that things did have a future between us, would the woman hate me? I'm getting too attached and I don't want to be heart broken when all this is over.

"What's wrong, Dani?" Millie asks. She's sitting next to me. This is the first time she hasn't been glancing around the limo in awe. Then again, that was me on the night of the hospital event.

I shake my head and paste on a smile. "Nothing. Just excited for tonight."

"Are you sure? You were texting and smiling and then you frowned. Is there anything I can do for you?"

"No, thanks. Miles said he was going to be a little late and I don't know, I guess I'm just excited to see him, you know?" The words are the truth and I swallow hard, trying to push back the tears. Why am I crying about him?

Millie smiles and taps my knee with her hand. "That's when you know it's love. When it's hard to be apart."

I laugh and say, "Where did you hear that?"

She shrugs. "I think my grandma said it first when I was young, but I've never had anything like that so I can't tell if it's true or not."

"No boyfriends?" I ask, trying to hide the full measure of my surprise.

Pink surges to Millie's cheeks and she shakes her head. "I come from a small town and the guys I was interested in weren't interested in me. The ones who asked me on a date were not my top picks either."

"I wish I could say you're missing out, but I'm not on the other side of the mountain yet."

"But you're engaged. That's promising, right?" Millie's words cause me to check myself. It's only fake after all.

With a quick nod, I say, "For sure. I mean, Miles is different than any of the guys I've dated before, which is a good thing."

Millie gives me a shy smile and asks, "How about kissing? Is he a good kisser?"

It's my turn to go lobster red and I nod. It's been a few days since we kissed and I'm pretty sure his kiss has turned the nerve-endings in my lips into live wires. Am I saying I can jumpstart a car with the amount of electricity flowing through them? Well, I'm not not saying it.

"What is it that makes it great?" Millie leans closer to me and the question is barely audible. I glance over at Evie and Kenzie who are facing each other. From a few words, I know Kenzie is filling Evie in on all the stats of the Boston Breeze. It's going to be rough talking her down from this high.

"Millie, have you never kissed anyone?" I whisper. My words make her face fall and I reach out, squeezing her hand in mine. "That's not a bad thing, girl."

She finally looks up and shakes her head. "Nope, I haven't been blessed with a first kiss."

I laugh, recalling my first kiss. "To be honest, waiting until later might be the best move. Maybe you'll find someone who makes you go weak in the knees with a kiss." Like Miles.

"Unless the guy thinks I'm a weirdo for never having kissed someone. I'll be awkward and, well, maybe I'll just stay away from guys."

I adjust in my seat so my body is angled toward her and say, "Not if he's the right guy. I mean, you've avoided the awkward, slobbery kisses of a teen guy. And any guy who makes fun of you for your lack of experience is probably a player anyway." Not a scientifical fact, but I've been through enough crappy relationships that it's a fair generalization. Enough as in two.

"So how does Miles compare to your ex-boyfriends?"

I laugh, turning the attention of Kenzie and Evie in our direction.

"What are we talking about over here?" Evie asks with a grin. And there might be some relief there about a change of subject.

"Comparing Dani's kisses," Millie says, sounding like she's never been more excited about anything in her life. The girl is only two years younger than me, but there's a big difference in life experiences.

Thank goodness the limo stops then, because I don't need this to get anymore awkward.

Walter lets us out right to the side of the arena. "Have a good evening, ladies."

"Thank you, Walter. This is amazing." I can't help but smile as the four of us walk up to the doors of the arena. The person scanning tickets takes a moment to scan all four and we're directed to the upper level.

"Maybe he's not as well connected as we think," Millie says.

Kenzie is positively shaking as we step onto the escalator. "No, he just knows people who can let us sit in a box."

My eyes go wide and I see a sign on the wall that says suites and the numbers. "No way." I told the guy not to pay for the tickets.

We enter suite one eighteen, but there's no company or family name on the outside to signal we're in the right place.

"Are you the friends of Miles?" a man asks, sitting on the small loveseat positioned next to the door.

I nod. "I'm Dani Higgins, his—" Thank goodness the man stops me because my brain goes almost blank.

"His fiancé. Yes." He stands up and shakes my hand. "Welcome. I'm Spencer, and Jack is over there." He points to a guy sitting in the chairs that face the ice.

Jack turns and I wave. "How are the stitches?" I ask.

He stands up and walks toward us. "They're almost done healing. We'll see what I look like after they're out. Maybe everyone will start calling me Frankenstein."

A hushed laughter comes from my roommates, and I take a step to the side so I can introduce them. "Jack and Spencer, these are my roommates, Kenzie, Evie, and Millie."

Spencer and Jack nod at everyone. But it's Jack who speaks for the crowd. "So, you made it to one of Trey's playoff games. It's supposed to be a good one."

Kenzie pushes me and Evie to the side, eager to hear more about this. "You know Trey?"

"Of course. He's one of our good friends. The Clark Group bought this suite once he signed with the Breeze."

And that must be how Miles got away with not buying the tickets for us. I'm still not sure why though. There must be plenty of clients wanting to be wined and dined in a fancy suite during the NHL playoffs.

The room has the loveseat where Spencer was sitting, as well as a small chair and coffee table next to it. Along the far wall is a countertop holding a large bowl of ice, and below it is a small refrigerator with a selection of drinks.

On the other wall is a small closet for jackets and a buffet-like counter, where several silver domes are set up.

A large table sits in the middle of it all and continuing forward, it opens into the seats that face the ice, which is where Jack sat a few moments ago.

Kenzie's body continues to vibrate with excitement and instead of talking like I thought she would, she takes several steps forward, dropping into one of the chairs to watch as the Zamboni drives around the ice.

"You'll have to excuse our Cave Woman over there," I say, pointing in Kenzie's direction. "She's one of the biggest fans of the Breeze I've ever met."

"That's not a bad thing," Spencer says, smiling wide.

Some people from catering come, dropping off what looks to be barbecue pulled meats. I wave for the girls to fill their plates, hanging to the side and checking my phone for a message from Miles.

Nothing. Hopefully he's okay.

"Worried about Miles?" Jack asks.

"Um, no, I just figured I'd check on some things for work." The excuse sounds lame to my own ears, but I smile and tuck my phone away.

Jack nods, as if he can read my thoughts. "He said he had to make a stop before heading here."

I don't know why that irritates me so much. It's not like we're in a real relationship and Jack knows it. But Miles has been so good about keeping me informed and guiding me through the entire process of his level of life, that I'm kind of hurt he didn't say anything when we texted earlier.

The Zambonis finish and the opening begins. A woman belts out the national anthem when I catch movement in my peripheral.

I turn to see Landon and Rachelle walk into the suite. "What are you two doing here?"

Landon juts his thumb over his shoulder and says, "Miles invited us. He figured it would be a good night to invite a bunch of people."

Rachelle smiles and says, "And guess who else is in town?"

I frown, not sure who she could mean. I turn to see Rachelle's sister Hillary walk in the door. With quick steps, I walk up and give her a hug.

"What are you doing back in Boston?" I ask, stepping away. The last time I'd seen her had been at our siblings' wedding to each other on a beautiful cliff that the bride had to take a chairlift to get to.

"I figured it was time. You can only live on a tropical island for so long. And pirate talk is fun and all, but after a week, I was over it." We laugh and she says, "We got a new boss and I decided it was time to come back and take part in the non-tourist crowd."

Millie turns around with wide eyes. "You lived on an island? How was that?"

Hillary turns and glances at Rachelle and then to Dani. "Definitely eye-opening."

About eight months ago, Hillary had been engaged to a man but had done a runaway bride act. Rachelle hadn't heard from her until the cruise, and then Hillary attended Landon and Rachelle's wedding. They'd had their rough moments, but it seems like things were starting to change to make Rachelle and Hillary closer.

The puck drops and I realize Miles is standing at the side, watching me. I walk over to him and wrap my arms around his waist. "Thank you."

"For what?"

"For inviting my brother and his wife."

I glance up as he shakes his head. "It wasn't a big deal. Landon mentioned how he'd love to go see a game some time, and I figured we could make it a party."

Something in his eyes causes my breathing to catch, and I wonder if he's feeling the same pull I am. Without thinking too long about it, I go up on tiptoes and kiss his cheek. His lips are only inches away and so tempting.

Spencer walks up to Landon, Rachelle, and Hillary, introducing himself and Jack. It's not until he motions toward Jack that Hillary says, "Jack Benson?" in a low voice.

I shrug, not knowing his last name. Miles steps forward and says, "Yes, do you know him?"

"Something like that." The way her eyes narrow, it's probably best to leave that topic of conversation alone.

I grab a plate of food and join Kenzie in the seats facing the ice, who is transfixed on the players skating below.

"Do you want something?" I ask, pointing to the food in my lap.

She turns, looking a little dazed and shakes her head when she sees me. The woman is usually into games, but bringing her to the actual arena has brought out a different side of her.

"Okay, so Carson Carver is number—" I begin.

"Eighteen. Trey is twenty-two, and Jason Styles is thirty-six."

"Who's Jason Styles?" I ask.

Kenzie turns to me, swiping a carrot from my plate and taking a bite. "The goalie."

I nod, acting like I totally knew that.

The game goes back and forth throughout the first period, the goalies playing amazing defense to keep the game scoreless. With only ten seconds left, the Breeze are on a breakaway but the goalie for the Sabers snags the puck with his glove.

And that rounds out the first period.

"What do you think?" I ask Kenzie.

"This is unreal. Probably the best night of my life."

"I'll take that as a compliment," Miles says, taking a seat next to me. Again, that heavenly cologne scent rushes my way and it's hard not to sniff the air.

"Are you getting a cold?" Miles asks, and my face turns at least ten shades redder.

I shake my head. "No, I just like the smell of your cologne."

He grins and focuses down on his plate. He also adjusts his legs and presses one up against mine. Um, is there such a thing as combustion in a person? Because all the emotions are building in that direction.

The second period goes by with no action, but the third period is a back and forth scoring match. When it comes down to the final few seconds, we're all standing as we wait to see what happens. I turn, burying my face into Miles's polo shirt, unable to watch.

He uses his hand to rub my back, and it's making it hard to keep my feelings from rising to the surface. A roar goes out amid the crowd, and I turn around, seeing the replay of the shot by Trey Hatch on the big screen.

Kenzie is near tears and I can only laugh. With the rest of the group here, it's the perfect night out. And the Breeze are one game away from winning the Stanley Cup.

"Are you riding in the limo with us?" I ask Miles, that hope rising in my chest.

Miles shakes his head. "Sadly, I drove. But I can send your brother and sister-in-law home in the limo and you can ride with me if you like."

Is that hope in his eyes?

I nod. "Sounds like a great plan."

"If you want, we can stick around and talk to Trey."

"Yes, please," Kenzie says, her eyes wide with excitement.

I shake my head and say, "Slow down, Tiger. The poor guy will have to put out a restraining order."

Our small group laughs but Kenzie brushes it off like it's no big deal.

"I'm not a stalker. Just an excited fan," Kenzie says.

We hang out in the suite for a while after the game and then head downstairs. After landing on the main level, Spencer guides us down through the lower level of the arena, talking to Millie.

Miles puts his phone to his ear and says, "Congrats, man." There's a pause and then he says, "We have a few people who want to meet you."

He slips his phone back into his pocket and replaces his hand around my waist, tugging me in closer to him. And I have to say I like it.

A few seconds later, a guy comes out of the tunnel below the rows of seats in a suit, his hair still wet.

"Hey all. I hear I've got a fan club. I'm Trey Hatch, nice to meet you all." He waves and makes his way through the door to reach us.

I glance over at Kenzie to see her reaction. Instead of the giddy excitement from moments ago, she's stoic, acting like this isn't a big deal for her. Man, the girl is a decent actress.

"I can sign some stuff for you if you want," Trey says, glancing around at us.

"That was a great game," I say, stepping out of Miles's grasp and reaching a hand out to Trey. "Congrats on the win."

Trey nods and smiles. "Thank you. We had some great shots. We're just lucky they fell in when they did."

I step back, nudging Kenzie with my elbow. Why isn't she talking?

She gives me a look that has me scurrying back to Miles.

Landon steps forward and starts chatting, but I'm focused on the guy next to me.

I shiver when he takes my hand, all the parts of electricity flowing through my fingers and palm. Why did I sign up for a fake relationship when this is the most chemistry I've ever felt? I'm going to have to tell him the truth, and soon. But would that make things awkward for his mother's event?

A few minutes later, the meeting with the hockey star is over and we head back up the stairs. Once we're walking out of the arena, I turn to Kenzie with my hand still in Miles's.

"What happened down there? You looked like a marble statue."

"They say don't meet your heroes," Kenzie mutters.

I frown, not sure what she means by that. "The guy seemed genuinely nice. Which is a big change to what I was expecting from a professional athlete."

"He just asks if he can sign something for us? How arrogant can you be?" Kenzie's face is twisted in a frown, and I have to hold back a laugh.

Before I can speak, Miles does. "Trey gets that a lot, to be honest. He was probably just trying to break the ice with that."

Kenzie turns to look at him and studies his face for a few moments before she nods.

We stop near the sidewalk with everyone chatting and recapping the game around us.

The limo pulls up along the curb and my roommates get in.

"We can go in the limo and leave the two of you the car, if that works," Rachelle says, winking at me.

"I was just about to suggest it," Miles says, squeezing my hand a couple times. They get in and the limo departs. Miles leads me in the direction of the parking garage.

"What did you think?" he asks me, pointing back toward the arena.

I grin. "That was amazing. Thanks for everything. And for putting up with all the people in my life."

His eyes are soft, and his lips turn up into a small smile. "It's refreshing to be around people who aren't all about angles and what they can get out of me." He chuckles a bit and says, "Kenzie had fun, huh?"

I laugh along with him and nod. "I'm sure we'll hear about it for the next several years."

"How are you doing?" he asks. We've stopped for a moment, and he's turned to face me. With the lights of the parking garage highlighting his face, I have to suck in a breath with how attractive he is at the moment.

"I'm good. Really good." A small voice in my mind is trying to warn me against something, but I'm too focused on the electricity flowing between us.

There's a moment when he moves forward a few inches, and my eyelids flutter, almost pleading for him to lean down and kiss me. He's almost there and then something in his eyes changes and he pulls back.

"I should get you home," he says. He still holds my hand, but he's not as relaxed as he was before.

Who am I kidding? The chances for my fake fiancé to fall in love with me were nonexistent from the start.

All I can think about is how I'm doomed for heartbreak.

CHAPTER 27
Miles

I t has been a long night of wanting to be close to Dani but also give her some space to hang out with her roommates. The balancing act of making our relationship believable isn't as hard as it was at the beginning, probably because Dani is the only person I think of on a daily basis now.

Walking her to the door, my brain runs through our first kiss, and I want so badly to lean down and kiss her again. I almost kissed her in the parking lot but remembered our rules of not showing PDA unnecessarily.

"What are you thinking about?" Dani asks, a sly smile on her lips.

"I'm wondering how you enjoyed the game." It's not the best coverup for my thoughts, but I don't need to freak her out.

She laughs and says, "We've talked about that a lot. It was great. I'm sure Kenzie will even say it was magical."

She's probably right about that. I've seen a lot of fans before, but Kenzie is definitely a die-hard Boston Breeze fan.

"Are you ready for the week?" I ask, reaching up and holding both of her upper arms.

After blowing out a breath, she nods. "I think so. Hit me with it. What do we need to attend now?"

"We have a few dinner meetings to attend, usually with clients. Next week is when we have two of the bigger events."

She nods, biting the side of her lip. I reach up and tip her chin up gently, making sure she looks me in the eyes. "What's wrong?"

"I'm like a bumbling idiot at these things."

I shake my head. "I think you did a great job at the last one. And for someone who hasn't grown up with it all, you're a natural. It was nice to have an excuse to leave though." For all the drama that night, Jack's doctor had done a great job. He'd probably come out with minimal scarring. But I'm still surprised his wound was so deep from a sharp bracelet.

Dani closes her eyes and nods, making the temptation to lean down and kiss her much harder. "I'll be fine when it gets here."

A car pulls up and we turn to see the limo stop next to the curb. This is my chance, so I tip her head back, leaning down and pressing my lips to hers. I use my arms to draw her in closer, and I'm surprised when she's holding just as tightly.

I've never enjoyed kissing someone this much. There's a hint of vanilla and the way we fit together just works.

Cheers ring out and we break apart to see her roommates walking up. "Looks like someone is winning tonight and it's not just the Breeze," Kenzie says, grinning at us.

"Leave them alone," Evie says, smiling as she walks past us and in through the front door.

Millie is all giggles as she follows the other two. We wait for them to close the door and then the porch light illuminates, causing us to laugh.

"I'll call you tomorrow," I say, trying to wrap up my growing feelings for the woman standing before me.

"Sounds good. Sleep well," Dani says, her eyes bright.

As I walk slowly back to my car, I know sleep probably won't be in my future. There's a woman I'm falling for, and she'll be the star of my dreams tonight.

CHAPTER 28
Dani

Watching Miles walk toward his car, I'm riding an emotional rollercoaster. I'm pretty sure he's the best kisser I've ever met. Like, I might be able to fly at this point from all the activity his kiss has started in my body.

Then there's the realization that he only kissed me when my roommates showed up, not when we were alone in the parking garage, so it's all for show.

But that was one of our rules, right? I shouldn't be getting mad about something we both agreed to. And the fact that he's keeping to it shows the kind of guy he is. He's a unicorn kind of guy. One that I thought was a myth until I met him.

I hate the rules.

Why can't I just lock my heart up and finish with our agreement? That would be the easiest and most pain-free way of getting through this. Maybe it would be easier if he wasn't thoughtful, or did things like invite my brother and his wife along to the hockey game.

I stride inside once his car is long gone, struggling to get up the stairs as all the energy has left me. Why am I acting like he just broke up with me rather than reveling in that amazing kiss?

I sit down on my bed and stare at the engagement ring on my

finger. My guess is it's a grandmother's or someone in the family. With this all being fake, why would he give me something that would probably mean a lot to his future wife?

Even the word in my brain has me wanting to cry. Because I don't have a chance of that title.

I curl up under my covers and try to breathe. I should've turned off the lights when I walked in, but they're still blazing above me, and I don't want to move.

"Good night," Kenzie says, as she walks past. Maybe if I'd been facing away from the door, she wouldn't have come in. "What's up?"

I force a smile. "It was a good night. Just trying to wind down."

She gives me a wide grin. "Um, it was a great night. If only I'd had someone to share a passionate kiss with like you," she says, poking me in the shoulder.

"Passionate? I don't know if we're to that point, or if we'll ever be."

"You obviously didn't have the angle I had," Kenzie says, winking.

We're silent a moment and tears well up, ready to fall.

"What's wrong, Dani? You're okay."

I sit up, wiping at my eyes. "It's just a lot, you know? I mean, the guy has like two faults and the rest of him is perfect."

Kenzie nods, her expression softening. "You're starting to have feelings for him, aren't you?"

I nod, the ball of tension in my throat making it hard to swallow, let alone talk.

"Maybe it's time to have a conversation about it then."

I shake my head. "Yeah, because rejection is my favorite thing in the world. That's all I've ever known from the men I've dated."

Kenzie reaches out a hand to take mine and squeezes a couple times. "Well, you only have a couple weeks left. It's either you talk to him about your feelings at some point, or you lose him completely."

I give her a fake smile and say, "Geez, you know how to make a girl feel better."

Instead of a retort back, Kenzie gives me a sad smile. "Take it from a girl who kept everything bottled up. The guy who proposed to me came back three days after the proposal and asked for the ring back, that he'd found someone who could love him completely. Who wouldn't fret in silence about things."

I reach forward, pulling Kenzie in for a hug. "I'm so sorry, Kenzie. That must've been awful."

She nods. "It's not easy being the product of parents who've both been married at least three times and hoping that marriage will be different for me. I guess that's why I wasn't as open as I should've been all those times."

I nod, cradling her as sobs take over. "When was this?"

"A year ago. I feel like I've been on one ride after another ever since."

"Well, you had some options there tonight," I say, trying to lighten the mood. "Maybe we should line you up with Trey."

Kenzie scoffs and shakes her head. "I don't think I'd survive as a hockey wife. They're always on the road or training. And what does a girl like me have to offer a guy like Trey?"

I reach over and rest my hand on her forearm, hoping to add some support. "Oh, girl. Everything. You could be the star of your own show if you wanted to be. Trey would be lucky to have you. You'll just have to get out more than two words." I smile, hoping she'll catch on that that last line is a joke.

"Someday I'll get back into dating. Just not now."

We sit in silence, and I think back to all that has happened since I met Miles. The wild ride I'm on wasn't expected at that time, but so far I've loved it. It's the future that's pressing down on me now, the unknown.

I need to tell him how I feel, but that's about as easy as handing him my heart and hoping he won't give it right back.

CHAPTER 29

Miles

The next two weeks go by like the tortoise running the race. It's probably because I haven't had a moment alone with Dani since dropping her off after the hockey game. With all the things she's had to arrange and get ready for the mixer and the dinners we've had to attend, there hasn't been much time to talk about anything else.

And for some reason, she hasn't been as open about life. Maybe that's just how she carries her stress.

So I call her. It's been a rough day dealing with my mother and I need to hear her voice. I'm like a sugar addict, needing just another bite of a doughnut or a candy bar.

"Hey, how's it going?" she says, and from the sound of her voice, she's got the phone pressed up against her ear to keep both hands free.

"It's going. My mother is fighting me over this project I had Oliver start on this week." I'm not sure what the motivation is, if she's still ticked that I'm engaged to Dani, but she's been trying to attack me at every angle.

Dani blows out a breath. "I'm sorry, Miles. Is there anything I can do?"

I smile, grateful for her willingness to help out. "You're already doing it."

"What do you mean?"

"I mean, hearing your voice helps soothe away some of that irritation."

She laughs and says, "My crazy voice makes you feel better. Oh buddy. You must be having a rough day."

"How goes everything for the mixer?"

"Great. I mean, I'm tangled up in strings of decorations at the moment, but at least I'll be able to finish this out and put the fear of my first mixer behind me." She pauses and says, "I convinced Jack to come. Hopefully he'll bring a few friends he mentioned."

Running a hand through my hair, I lean back in my desk. It's only four p.m. on a Friday, but I'm ready to be done.

"Do you need help with the set up?"

"I'll never turn down help. We're in the CFA building. Come when you can."

I end the phone call and log off my computer, knowing this will help me a lot more than sitting around in my office.

As I drive over to Boston University, I mentally go through the meeting I'd had that morning with my mother. She's been difficult ever since the whole engagement thing happened, but it's like she's trying to get me to bend to her will by being a thorn in my side.

And at this point, I'm over it. I don't want to be in her control forever.

This idea I had in working with Oliver is like breathing new life into my work persona. I've been so bored for so long, just doing what my mother asks of me that I haven't thought outside the box or worked on something that gets me excited to go to work every day.

And as much as I don't want to, maybe it's time to step away from the company. There has been a lot of turnover in the past two years as it is, many people getting fed up and leaving because of my mother's dictatorship. It might be something to talk over with Oliver. He obviously believes in this project enough to work on it himself, but will that work if I end up having to fund it out of my own pocket?

From the stories of Dani and others who've been on the receiving end of healthcare, if I can help make the weight of it all a bit easier, I want to do that. It might take some time, but this is a cause worthy of pursuing.

These thoughts get me all the way to BU, and I'm ready for a distraction. I walk through the building where I'd had one class forever ago, and I swear everything still looks and smells the same. It's like a mixture of ink and mildew.

I stand next to the door, taking in the scene of the room. There are hundreds of hanging lights crisscrossed from wall to wall around the nine-foot mark. There are several tall tables spread with a floor-length tablecloth on the far end and regular height tables with white tablecloths closer to me.

With a million decorations in other spots around the room, I stop looking as I find my girl.

I mean, not *my* girl, but the one I came here to see. Obviously.

"Hey," Dani says, walking up to me with a smile. She leans up and gives me a quick kiss, which has me stunned where I stand. We're not anywhere that we need to prove our relationship, but I'll take it.

"Hey yourself." I pick up a section of thick beads she's got wrapped around her neck and laugh. "Please tell me these are Sonia approved."

She laughs, the sound cutting right to my chest and ripping away some of the anxiety. "These are an early birthday gift from my sister, Sami. I might have to run it by Sonia if I decide to wear it to your mom's thing next weekend."

"How can I help?" I ask, glancing around the large room. I'd had a few conferences and meetings here since graduation, but it had been a while and with the decorations, it already looks different. "Are you prepping for a high school dance?"

Dani shrugs. "Well, I'm trying something different this time.

I've gone over the notes for past mixers and am hoping to make things a little more exciting."

"You're going to do games and stuff, aren't you?" I say, rolling my eyes.

She hits me with a light jab to the shoulder. "Yes, yes I am. And you'd better be helping people with it, seeing as you're my fiancé." Her cheeks color and she turns around quickly, probably to cover up the fact she didn't add fake to the beginning.

That gives me a shred of hope, but there's still that lingering doubt that maybe she really is just in it for the agreement to help each other. I've been used before, but I don't think I've wanted something as much as I need to know her feelings.

The two other people who'd helped us set things up have already left by the time we wrap up two hours later. I'm happy we're not pulling an all-nighter to get this thing ready.

Standing back, I nod. "This is simple, but classy."

"Thank you," Dani says. Her beaming smile has my stomach doing gymnastics.

"Where would you like to eat?" I ask, my stomach rumbling in response.

She shakes her head. "I'm not picky. Is there somewhere you recommend for under fifteen dollars?" With a laugh, she says, "Our paychecks were delayed until Monday."

I shake my head. "You're not going to need money. I'm buying."

Blowing out a breath, Dani says, "Miles, I owe you so much already. You don't need to buy me dinner. Let's go to one of the chain restaurants."

"No, I think I know of a place."

We head outside and I take her hand in mine, loving the feel of her inner strength and the idea of it being like this forever. Tanya had never loved the physical touching in public, and now I can understand that I need it. The strength I've been able to gain from Dani, not in a magical woo-woo sense, but in a supportive situation, has been so important.

"So, is everything okay with you and your mom?" she asks.

I blow out a breath, not sure how much I should unload on Dani. "Not really. There's a lot that goes into her personality. I think one thing she's having a hard time with is control. I don't do everything she says now and with this new research I'm working on with Oliver, I think she's worried I'll leave."

"Is that what you want?" Dani asks, glancing up at me.

"It's a thought. I mean, if she's never going to retire, I might have to find or start something else in order to do what I love."

"So, you don't want to be CEO?" Her question has me turning to inspect her expression. Is she hoping that's what I'll become? Because she's never worried about that or money before. But really, we're getting close to the end of our fake relationship and I might be reading too much into every little thing.

I shrug. "Again, I don't know. I mean, my life has been dictated in so many ways since I was a small child, that the freedom of not worrying about her disappointment is addicting."

Dani lays her free hand on my arm and gives it a small pat. "I can only imagine how hard that's been. But ultimately, you're the one who has to live with you. And you can always set the boundaries necessary to keep you sane."

I glance down at her and wonder what she's thinking. "Do you have experience with that?"

She gives me a sad smile. "I didn't realize it until after the fact, but yeah. I should've spoken up a lot more about my feelings and what I wanted when I was with Clay. Hopefully I'll recognize when I need to set boundaries in the future."

We change topics and head into a small diner tucked into a side-street near the campus. It's been a while since I've been here and I'm glad they're still open late.

"What's this place?" Dani asks, pointing toward the restaurant.

"It's the reason I graduated with a bachelor's. I couldn't study in the library because it was too quiet, and doing anything productive with my roommates distracting me was near impossible. This little diner is the perfect blend of commotion but zero people wanting to talk to me every five minutes."

She laughs and the sound sinks into my chest. I hold onto it for an extra second as it turns into a longing I haven't felt before.

"I would've been the distractor. I had to lock myself away in my room to get anything done."

One of the servers, Stacy, guides us to a small table and I smile, trying to picture Dani stuck in her room. Everywhere we've gone together, she learns the names of people and remembers them, no matter their job.

"Hi Stacy," she says, glancing down at the menu again. "I'm going to get the bacon cheeseburger combo. And can I get ranch on the side?"

"Of course," Stacy says, taking the menu from her. I give my order and turn to Dani.

"Ranch on the side? What is that?"

Dani's eyes go wide. "Have we not had a chill meal since our fake relationship began?" She blinks a couple times and shakes her head. "Ranch is my weakness. Fries, pizza, garlic bread."

I laugh, thinking how we've been fake dating for six weeks and we've only had nicer meals in all that time.

"You can't just use ketchup?" I say, teasing.

"No. That's not an option." She takes a sip from her glass of water and then says, "One of my roommates was from Idaho. They have this weird thing called fry sauce, which is basically ketchup and mayo mixed together. Now that's weird."

I'd heard about fry sauce but never had the chance to try it.

"Are you ready for tomorrow night? What else can I help you with?" I ask, studying her reaction. She's glancing away, but I can see the pull of tension around her mouth.

"I'm about as ready as I can be. I mean, I've never actually been to one of these things, so I'm not sure how well it will go."

Leaning back against the padded booth backrest, I smile. "Well, usually there is some kind of introduction section. The last few I've attended have me fill out a nametag so people know who I am."

"Always a good idea," Dani says, nodding.

"Then whoever is conducting will share what the needs are of whatever charity they're trying to fund, or just let us mingle to get to know others."

Dani leans forward, her eyes locking onto mine. "How often have you actually met someone at a mixer that you interacted with after the event?"

"Quite a few, actually. It helps to go in with a purpose of why I'm there and I usually connect with someone who can help me, or I can help them."

She sits back and nods. "That gives me hope. I was beginning to question whether all of this is worth it."

"You're doing a great job. Hopefully the turnout of people shows it."

Our meal goes by faster than I want it to, but at least she's letting me take her home. As we get closer to the house, I glance down at the ring on her finger, surprised she's still wearing it.

But why wouldn't she? This is the arrangement after all.

"We really need to come up with a story about our proposal, don't we?"

Dani nods, giving me a surprised look. "That would be for the best. We've been able to skirt around it for the past few dinners with general ideas, but going to your mom's event would probably be easier to convince people with an elaborate story. Or at least something on the same page."

Instead of turning down the road that leads to her house, I pull to the side of the road for a moment, opening a new text message to an old friend. Once that's sent, I veer to the left and head toward the river.

"Where are we going?" Dani asks and I have to smile, coming up with the plan as I drive.

"We're almost there."

The night is dark, but with the lights of the city, we can see something. And with it being past midnight, there aren't as many cars out. I park and walk around to open her door.

Her eyes show the confusion and I take her hand in mine, liking how we fit together so well.

I lead her around the corner as Fenway Park opens up.

"What are we doing here?" she asks.

"We're getting that story." I lead her around to where the players come into the field and knock. It takes a few seconds before the door opens but a man I've known for several years stands there with a smile on his face.

"Mr. Clark. It's good to see you."

"You too, Ralph. Do you mind if we go on the field for a couple minutes?"

The man glances at his watch. "We just finished cleaning up for the night. I can give you five minutes max. I need to get home to the wife."

I turn to Dani, who looks like she's just been turned into a Greek statue. With a tug on her hand, we follow Ralph through the tunnel to get to the Red Sox dugout.

"How do you know Ralph?" Dani asks in a whisper.

"Mr. Clark here," Ralph says, pointing to me, "Helped my kid get a kidney a couple years ago. And saved my job here after taking all the time off for treatments."

"That's really cool," she says, something different in her voice.

We step out onto the neatly trimmed grass and Ralph disappears into the shadows. A moment later, the lights that illuminate the seats behind the plate turn on.

"May I have the ring, m'lady."

Dani gives me a small smile before slipping the ring off her finger. Her posture is rigid and there's something in her eyes I can't read. As soon as she hands me the ring, she turns around, walking around home plate.

That's not how my proposal plan had worked out in my mind on the drive over here.

I stick the ring into my pocket and casually walk behind her, the realization of why we're here hitting me. Maybe I should've just pulled over and got down on one knee in front of her house. But that's not how I've ever pictured proposing.

And even with the little planning, I still want to make this memorable. I'm just wishing it wasn't under false pretenses.

CHAPTER 30

Dani

C ue the freak out. I can't believe I'm standing on the grass of Fenway Park. Secondly, the reason we're here has me acting like a robot.

I walk around home plate, thinking of all the players I've watched over the years as they've walked on this field. Fenway Park was one of my dad's favorite places. We would get tickets for out in right field and spend a few hours watching our favorite team play a several times a year.

Thinking of my dad heightens my emotions already and then thinking of the very attractive man striding close behind me throws it over the edge.

I finally turn, wishing on so many levels that this experience could be real, that I could be getting engaged to this man and planning out our life together.

Miles Clark, heir to the Clark Group is standing here with me getting ready to propose. Yeah, there's no way this would happen in my real life.

"What's wrong?" Miles asks, stepping forward to take my hands in his.

I shake my head, trying to put on the perfect smile. "Nothing.

I mean, I've never been able to walk on the field, so it's kind of a lot." And wishing his proposal could be real.

Miles smiles down at me and nods. "I know you like this place and figured it would be a good spot to create our story."

My brain hitches on "our" for way longer than it should.

Reaching into his pocket, Miles sinks down onto one knee, the lights from behind me causing him to blink a few times.

"Danielle Higgins—"

"Sophie." I pause a second and say, "Danielle Sophie Higgins."

This might be the only proposal I ever get. I might as well make it daydream worthy.

The corner of Miles's mouth turns up and he begins again. "Danielle Sophie Higgins. I know we've had an unconventional relationship, but you're pretty amazing. You are a one-of-a-kind woman and someone I get excited to be around. Would you do me the honor of becoming my fiancé?"

I nod, processing the words as he slips the ring onto my finger. The speech was great, but did he mean any of it? And using fiancé shows the eventual decline of our relationship. Eventual as in next week.

Strike number forty for me, reminding me I shouldn't have accepted this fake relationship anyway.

Staring down at the ring, I swallow hard, wishing I could block out all the emotions surging.

Miles stands and pulls me into a hug. The smell of him, the strength of his embrace, and the atmosphere of where we are causes a tear to fall.

He pulls back and glances at my face for a second before leaning in. His lips press against mine and suddenly I can feel every nerve in my body sparking to life. His arms around my waist tug me closer, and while my brain is trying to warn me about the consequences of more contact with him, my heart is staging a rebellion.

Someone clears their throat behind us, and we break apart to see Ralph grinning at us. "Sorry to interrupt, but it's been five minutes, Mr. Clark."

Miles nods and turns away, slipping his hand into mine. Everything about this night feels real, like to the part I might have slipped past crush territory and right into the depths of the love pool.

And my heart now has a timer, ticking away until this all ends for me.

CHAPTER 31

Miles

I'm lucky if I got two hours of sleep the night before. My brain had gone through every interaction with Dani, trying to figure out what was off about her. She'd been fine at the diner, and everything was normal until we arrived at Fenway. Our kiss was the moment that had her relaxed, and I have to say, it was one for the books. Even better than the previous ones we've shared.

Me: How did you sleep?

That easy way of talking had been gone once I dropped her off at her house, and while she claimed she was just tired after a long day, I worry that something has changed.

Well, we did have a very real-feeling proposal, to the point that I had goosebumps going up and down my spine when it happened.

Dani: Not well. I got the play-by-play of last night's Boston Breeze game from Kenzie.

I laugh, remembering Kenzie's enthusiasm in the suite at the hockey game but her stoic expression when she met Trey. That would be an interesting relationship.

Me: Can I bring you something this morning?

I could swing by a bakery or coffee shop and take her breakfast before she has to leave for the university.

Dani: Thanks, but I'm already out the door. There's still a lot to get ready.

Me: Good luck.

Dani: I won't need it as long as you're there.

Some of the tension in my chest eases up a bit, and I grin. Things are getting complicated between the two of us, but nothing feels as right as being around and with Dani.

Several hours later, I swing by and pick up Jack and Trey, who'd started his career playing for Boston University.

"Okay, Miles, what are we in for?" Trey says from the back seat. I half-expected him to show up in jeans and one of his hockey jerseys, which would be a lot like our days in college.

"From everything I've heard from Dani, this mixer is to help support the school. If it goes well for her, she'll be able to keep her job."

Trey shakes his head. "No pressure, right?"

Jack and I glance at each other before laughing. "You do know that's your entire career, right?" Jack says.

He shrugs. "Yeah, but at least I have some control over it. Getting canned for people not opening their wallets to donate? That sucks."

We drive a bit and Trey says, "So, how are things going with Dani, anyway? I wish I'd been there when Jack started messaging the girl on the dating app. And getting you to fake date. It's like I miss all the good stuff while I'm on the ice."

I turn a quick glare at Jack before focusing back on the road.

"Don't give me that look," Jack says, chuckling. "Spence spilled the beans."

Trey slaps my shoulder and says, "It's all good, bro. This way you've escaped the matchmaking expertise of Mama Hatch."

That makes me smile. "Is she trying to get you to date someone?"

"I think you mean several someones." Trey shakes his head

and leans back against the back seat. "It doesn't matter where I go, she's tried to set me up with women almost daily. Something about needing grandbabies in her life. I need to get a new routine and forget to tell her."

We make it to the parking lot and park, noting several other nice cars around us.

The three of us make it into the building, walking up to the table to check in. There are the obligatory name badges, but I'm not as bugged to wear them this time because I know how hard Dani has worked to make this night a success.

"Here is a schedule of the night's events," a woman says, handing us a few papers. "Should you like to donate back to the university at any point tonight, please speak with Sharon Tillotson."

We take a few steps away and Trey leans over, keeping his voice low when he says, "I guess at least they're not trying to hide the fundraising efforts."

I nod and continue on, glancing around the room for a familiar face I've been hoping to see all day.

"There's your fiancé," Jack says, leaning over and pointing toward the far wall. I don't know why the word sounds different today, maybe because I actually proposed last night. But from the pinched look, I know she's in need of some help.

"I'll catch up with you guys in a few." I turn and walk toward Dani, ignoring the teasing sounds the two guys make behind me.

I reach over and touch her elbow lightly, not wanting to scare her to death. "Hey, how's it going?"

Dani shakes her head. "It's been a day. The caterer called in sick earlier today so it's been an adventure trying to get everything ready for tonight. I was tempted to buy the stuff for Rice Krispie Treats and peanut butter sandwiches. But the gal we were able to get has been amazing."

"Who is it?" Not that I'm the one to do the scheduling of catering events, but I'm curious who she was able to get on short notice.

"A gal Tiffany, my sister-in-law's cousin, recommended. The Love, Austen company she works for has used her for several events. From everything I've seen in there, she does a great job. I just hope tonight goes well."

"Love, Austen? Isn't that a matchmaking company?" My brain goes back to the woman Jack texted what feels like forever ago.

Dani nods. "Yeah."

I'm curious about whether or not Dani has ever logged into something like that, but it's not the right time for that discussion.

I lean forward, wrapping an arm around her and pulling her close. She melts into me and I'm okay for a few minutes of this. Okay, I'd be fine standing this close and practically cuddling all night.

"You're doing a great job. What do you need from me?"

She gives me a small smile. Lifting her hand to brush a wisp of hair back, she says, "For now, just smile and make the rounds. Encourage people to donate." Her smile widens with that remark, and I have to laugh, hoping she'll be able to get past some of the stress of the night and enjoy what she's put together.

"That I can do." As if totally natural, I lean forward, brushing my lips against hers. I don't know how she does it, but my brain goes fuzzy after contact.

I grab a soda from the table, knowing that a clear head is best since I'll be driving home. The man next to me comments about the lack of napkins on the table and I see someone walking over with a stack of them in hand.

After a quick survey of the room, I take in a deep breath, prepping myself for the many conversations to come.

I'm used to going to these things when I'm forced to and in a sense I'm obligated to attend now. But I want to do it for Dani, to help in whatever capacity I can.

There is a small group around one of the taller tables and I walk over to join. A wave of panic crosses through me at the fact I know nothing about these people, but remembering the times

Dani has helped me center myself gives me a little more footing to stand on.

My best strategy is to take this like a research lesson at the beginning. Because if my brain thinks I'm cataloging information for later, I tend to avoid the severe panic attacks.

I walk up, listening to the conversation there. One of the two men is talking, waving his arms as he tells his story. The women and other man seem to be eating it up.

"I'm under this pile of ten guys and know that if I don't move them off me, my rib is going to puncture my lung. I take in one more deep breath and push up, nearly lifting the guys off the ground."

That's when a red flag pops up in my brain. The guy is probably showing off, so I give him the benefit of the doubt.

"The guys in New Zealand were really chill. And because of my injuries, the airline bumped me up to first class all the way back to Boston."

"I doubt they'd do a complimentary bump to first class for injuries." The moment the words are out of my mouth, I regret saying them. But the way this guy is going off, he needs to be stopped.

The guy's head swivels toward me and his eyes narrow. "Who are you?"

"Miles. I'm just saying that I've done a lot of international travel and they don't usually give you a free pass to the front of the plane."

The others around the table are shifting like they're uncomfortable, all except for the other guy, who looks like he's about to open presents on Christmas.

"Obviously I would know, having just lived through it." The guy points to the boot on his foot and I shake my head.

"Why do you have a boot if your injury was to your ribs?" I need to just let this go, but something about the braggart irritates me. Maybe it's the captive audience he has or that his story is over-the-top.

"Wait," one of the women says, pointing toward me. "Aren't you Miles Clark?" The excitement in her eyes makes me want to disappear.

I nod. "That's me."

"I'm Lauren Wales," the woman says, sticking out her hand. "I had economics with Professor Rob, and he always talked about you. It's nice to finally meet you."

"You too. What do you do, Lauren?" I ask, sipping on my drink.

"I work for Goldman Sachs."

I nod, smiling at her. "That awesome. Congrats."

"Working for Deloitte is probably a dream come true," Boot Guy says.

Instead of acknowledging the guy, I turn to look at the other three on the table. I might as well jump right into the conversation and see how we can all help each other. "Where do you all work?"

The man dips his head a bit and shakes it. "I'm Paul Donohue. The company I was working for just downsized."

I swallow, a mound of guilt rising up to my throat. In a city as expensive as Boston is and with a partner, being laid off has to be difficult.

"What is it you did before?" I ask, leaning against the table.

"Research. I worked for one of the tech divisions here in Boston."

I nod. "What kind of tech?"

"Configuring all the parts and then testing them out. They fazed out our entire division when they bought machines to do that work." The man pauses for a moment and shakes his head. "Don't they realize they're going to need humans to fix the machines that make the machines?"

"We've got a research team up and running on some new tech for the hospitals. Here's my card," I say, pulling it from my suit coat's inner pocket. "Give me a call on Monday and I'll set up an interview."

The man looks up, his jaw dropping as he's dumbfounded. "Really?"

"For sure, Paul. Everyone deserves a second chance."

I glance around the table and catch the nametag on Mr. Boot Leg's jacket. Clay.

Why does that sound familiar? It's not too common, but I know I've heard it recently.

He must be trying to figure out who I am as well. "Miles Clark. Rich daddy and mommy, right?"

I give him a fake smile and shake my head. "Knowledge of work isn't something I lack."

"Didn't you just get engaged?" Lauren asks. Her gaze bounces from my face to something or someone behind me and I turn, seeing Dani walking in my direction.

"How's it going over here?" she asks, standing with a few inches to spare next to me.

Lauren's eyes widen and she says, "She's your fiancé, right?"

Dani's cheeks go a bright pink and she nods, smiling. She glances up at me and then over at the other people along the table.

It's then the smile drops and all the color drains from her face.

"Danielle?" I turn to see Clay hobbling to the side of the second tall table and things are starting to click. This is her ex-boyfriend?

"Clay. I didn't know you'd be here." Her words have an edge to them.

Clay shrugs and gets closer, reaching out a hand to touch Dani's arm. "It was time, honey bear. And I thought I'd run into you here."

Dani takes a step back and frowns. "Please don't cause a scene." From the way her voice drops so only Clay and I can hear, I know she's nervous.

"I think it's time for you to go, Superman." Clay glances at me, trying to figure out what I mean by that.

He shakes his head. "No, I'm right where I need to be. Danielle and I belong together."

She scoffs and shakes her head, her arms folded tightly around her waist. "You're the one who broke things off, Clay, by dating Amber."

I turn to see if Dani is serious, a bunch of pieces clicking together. No wonder she was irritated with Amber when we first met. The woman had stolen her ex-boyfriend.

"The chances of you being with this guy are slim. Is she paying you to be here?" Clay asks, turning to face me.

"Why would you say that? No. I'm here because I want to be." I take another step so I'm between Dani and Clay, looking down at him with the most intimidating face I can muster.

"She's not worth it, man. And to propose after a few weeks of dating? You must be desperate."

Before my brain can take control of my nervous system, my fist is flying through the air, connecting with Clay's cheekbone. My knuckles tingle with pain, but some of my frustration is gone.

Dani stands frozen, as if trying to figure out what just happened.

A woman with brown curly hair runs over. "What's going on here? What's the meaning of this?"

Clay points at me. "This guy hit me. Threw a punch right near my eye. I'm going to have damage there now. You'll see me in court, man."

What a weasel.

"You deserved it after talking to Dani like that." The room is quiet, everyone looking in our direction.

"I'm going to have to ask you to leave, sir." The woman's hand points in the direction of the door, and my stomach sinks. I'm here to help Dani, not make her life harder.

I nod my head. "How about I stay away from this guy and I'll be over here. I was planning on donating some money to the cause."

"The other guy was being a tool," Paul says, in my defense.

Sharon glances at Paul, then to me, and back down to Clay, who's acting like a soccer player who flopped to get the call. Don't get me wrong, I like soccer, but right now, I despise Dani's ex-boyfriend.

"Fine, stay away from each other for the remainder of the night." She turns to Dani, who's still statuesque, and frowns. "What is the problem? Why couldn't you handle this?"

Her mouth quivers and she says, "It's personal."

"Get it together. You know how much this night means to your job and mine." The woman walks away and Dani, one of the strongest people I've ever met, looks like she's about to crumble.

I step closer, pulling her into my arms. "Hey, it's all right. I'm sorry about that."

She nods her head against my chest and takes in a deep breath. We stand like that for another couple seconds and then she steps back. "Okay, I have to pull myself back together and lead out the rest of the event."

Without glancing back, she steps away.

"She's not your type, man."

I glare at Clay and say, "Don't tell me who's my type." I take a giant step over him. He flinches, as if I'm planning to step on him and I walk away, trying to put into place my feelings as I reconcile the guy on the floor with Dani and how their relationship had managed to last over five years.

My heart has been falling for Dani over the past couple weeks and Clay's statement still rings in my ears as I cross the room to join Jack and Trey. Of course, the guy is a tool anyway, but what does he know about Dani that I don't?

CHAPTER 32
Dani

By the end of the event, I was dragging. Seeing Clay there had thrown me for a loop and then when Miles hit him, I felt a mixture of both pride and panic, knowing that this could've ruined the entire event.

We received quite a few sizeable donations by the end of the night, and Sharon seemed pleased, so maybe there is some hope for us yet.

It's a few days later and I feel like I've finally recovered emotionally and physically from the stress and exhaustion. Maybe I'm not cut out for event planning.

And now, here I am back at the expensive mall waiting for Sonia to bring the final dress to me. Miles said he'd come with me, but after everything that's happened, I've just needed some space to think.

I really like the guy, practically love him. But Clay's words seem to reopen wounds I thought were healed every time I think about it.

What would Miles see in me? I mean, this coming weekend is the tipping point of our relationship. The end of our contract. And it all just fills me with dread.

My phone rings and my mother's name pops up on the

screen. "Hey Mom," I say, glancing around the room for Sonia. I'm not in the mood to talk about anything right now, and sometimes my mom can go on and on about things.

"Hey Dani-girl. What are you up to?"

"I'm here getting fitted for a dress for this weekend. Miles's mom is throwing a big party we're attending." My heart is cracking all over again as I realize how many lies have gone into this relationship.

"That sounds so fun. I'm sure you'll look beautiful. What color is the dress?"

I try to remember from the fitting we had several weeks ago. "I think it's like a magenta, or a teal color."

"Dani, I hate to tell you, but those are two completely different colors." She's chuckling and I can't help but join in.

"I know, Mom. It's been a while since I saw it."

"Well, I don't want to keep you too long, I just thought I'd call and see if you're free at the end of August. I think it's the twenty-eighth."

I frown, confused since my mom usually just invites me to things instead of seeing if I'm available.

"I don't think I have anything. Why?"

"Your sisters and I thought we'd throw you a bridal shower. Sami's already designed the invitations, we just wanted to see if you had any other fancy events before we start sending them out."

I swallow hard, fighting back the tears that surge. It's all too real in my life, all except for the pretense of being Miles's future wife.

I swipe at the tears and nod. "Um, I'll have to check and get back to you. Hold off on sending anything out just yet."

"Sounds good. Let me know after this weekend so we can get the ball rolling."

We say our goodbyes and right now I wish I wasn't sitting in the main part of the mall. Things had seemed so easy at the beginning and now every thing is a complicated mess.

"Okay, Dani," Sonia says, carrying a garment bag. "Let's get you ready for the ball."

I laugh, the sound coming out more like the hee-haw of a donkey after all the silent heartache flooding through me. It doesn't take long for the dress to go on and for me to step out for inspection.

"You look absolutely beautiful," Sonia says, walking in a circle around me. I stare into the mirror, taking in the teal color of the dress. It's got gems and sequins throughout, the neckline rising to my throat and the fabric reaching the edge of my shoulders. The dress goes to the floor, the heavier fabric draping the rest of my body. I'm amazed at how this one piece can fit so well.

I take in shallow breaths, trying to make my head and my heart stop fighting over all that's going on in my life. I just need to make it through this weekend. Then I can dissolve into a puddle of tears and hopefully, eventually laugh at what my life has come to.

"Thank you, Sonia."

She walks over and takes my hands in hers. "Miles is a lucky man to have someone like you at his side."

I shake my head, the tears threatening to flow again. "I don't know if I'm cut out for all this."

Sonia frowns. "You'll be fine. You're so strong and Miles can't stop talking about how great you are."

"He can't?" I step down from the small platform where I've been modeling the dress and Sonia helps me undo the back before I walk into the dressing room again.

"He was just in here this morning getting his tux ready. Apparently he took out your ex-boyfriend?" She smiles, her eyes practically dancing.

I laugh, feeling a small release from everything that's happened over the past several days. "That he did. He talked to you about all this?"

"Of course. He likes to chat while we get him ready for events.

I think it's hard when his mom doesn't listen like he wants her to."

Her words echo in my brain a few times as I change back into my jeans and blouse.

"Thank you, for everything, Sonia." It feels almost like a forever goodbye and my heart squeezes.

"Of course. Let me know when you're in need of some more clothes. We start going through the fall wardrobes in a couple weeks and I can get you all set up."

I walk out with the dress bag on my arm and tears streaming down my cheeks. As amazing as this experience has been, even with the few bumps along the way, I'm going to miss it.

Not the stuff, per se, but the guy. I finally find Mr. Right and there's a chasm between us. That's my luck though.

Better move on, Dani.

But how?

CHAPTER 33
Miles

The week between the mixer and the gala has been one of the longest in my life. I've wanted to spend all my time with Dani, but with all the research happening for the new monitor, I've had to spend most of my time in meetings.

I sent flowers to Dani's house and tried to stay in contact as much as possible, but I think going to the gala tonight will help since I'll be able to talk to her face-to-face.

The ride to her house feels like forever but I'm finally here, standing on the doorstep.

When the door opens, I see Evie's face, her expression tight as she gives me a small smile.

"Everything okay?" I ask, hoping Dani isn't hurt or worse.

"It will be, I hope," she says, opening the door.

I step into the house and there's something I can't place. Dani comes down the steps, looking like a vision with her hair curled on top of her head and the dress bringing out the color of her eyes. But there's a sadness there and all I want to do is get rid of it.

"You are beautiful," I say, waiting until she's close to me to say the words.

She gives me a bashful smile and says, "Thank you."

"Are you ready?" I ask, holding out my arm for her.

She nods and slips her hand through. With a quick goodbye, we're out the door as we walk toward the limo.

"How was your day?" I ask, hoping to spark some kind of conversation with her.

It isn't until we're settled inside that she turns to me, tears glazing her eyes and ready to spill out.

"Not that great. I feel like I've been through the ringer this week."

I reach over and take her hand, hoping to infuse some support. "What's going on?"

"Well, my boss called this morning to say that with everything that happened at the mixer last weekend, they're relieving me of my position. Apparently a mix-up of personal business isn't allowed."

She turns to look through the small clutch she brought, pulling out a tissue.

"That's ridiculous. You lost your job because of me?"

With a quick shake of her head, she blows out a breath, her body shaking as if it's a lot of work to relax. "I'm guessing it was Clay. He has a way of getting back at people when he's slighted."

"I've been waiting for charges all week from him," I say. Not exactly waiting for them, since work has taken a lot of my time, but I didn't think he'd hurt Dani. "I'll make some calls and get it fixed."

She places her hand on my arm and gives it a quick squeeze. "No, I'll take care of it. I mean, after tonight we'll be navigating whatever comes next. I'll figure something out. I always manage to land on my feet."

The last few minutes of the ride are quiet and I'm going through every scenario to help fix the situation. Getting her fired is not what I wanted to have happen and causing Dani any more pain is killing me.

We step out to see the Boston Park Plaza all lit up. Inside, the décor my mother's event planner put together, the whites and golds pulling in all the room and making everything bright.

"This place is beautiful." Dani glances up in awe, and I can't help but watch her face.

"Thank you for being here with me tonight. I promise, I will help make things right."

She gives me a small smile. "Really, Miles. It will be okay. If you hadn't punched Clay, I know he would've found some other reason to get me in trouble. Let's go get this party started."

There's a small glimpse of the woman I'm falling in love with, but then again, I shouldn't expect her to be overly happy and witty all the time. She's strong and I can use her in my life. Permanently. I'll have to find a way to tell her that by the end of the night.

The moment I'm inside, I'm pulled away by a couple of men who've been connected to the Clark Medical Group almost since it began. Spencer walks up and takes my place next to Dani, helping her navigate the room. It doesn't matter what the conversation is at the moment, it's like I've got a Dani radar telling me where she is at all times.

Only three hours to go until we can talk about furthering our relationship.

CHAPTER 34
Dani

As if the first event I attended six weeks ago wasn't crazy enough, this one seems like it has an unlimited budget. Maybe that would've helped me save the mixer.

I shake my head. Now is not the time to think about what I could've done differently. Sharon was apologetic in her phone call and even said how grateful she was to have worked with me. But I didn't think I'd be jobless this soon after graduation.

"Okay, Miss Dani," Spencer says, walking next to me. "How about we get a drink to start off this night?"

"You make me sound like a preschool teacher," I say, laughing. I haven't spent a whole lot of time around Spencer, but he's been a nice chaperone tonight. Miles looked as though he didn't want to leave me alone, but said he'd be back soon. At least I know someone else here.

"Well, I mean, you're helping out Miles."

That hurts, making me realize just how close we are to the end. I glance over at Miles, who looks distracted as he's talking to the people he needs to.

I'm so focused on him that I don't see who's in front of me until Spencer nudges me with his arm.

"This is, um, Miles's mom, Anita Clark. This is Dani, Miles's fiancé."

The woman's lips are pinched together and I'm not sure whether to laugh or cry at this situation.

"It's so nice to finally meet you," I say. Okay, maybe that was a little too much brightness for this woman. "Miles was talking about having dinner with you at some point."

"I'm sure he was," the woman says drily. "Spencer, I'm going to need a minute with Miss Higgins."

I turn to glance at him, hoping he won't leave me here by myself, but he nods, giving me a concerned look.

"Follow me," Mrs. Clark says. She turns on her heel and practically marches to the doors. I feel like I'm being led to my execution with how this is all playing out.

With a quick glance behind, I see Spencer following at a distance. What is it about this woman that has Miles and all his friends terrified?

We walk through the ornate doors and into an empty hallway. Mrs. Clark whirls around, causing me to jump from the sudden action.

"I'm not sure what your intentions are with my son, but know that you'll never live up to his expectations."

I frown, the frustration that has been building over the past several days coming to the surface. "Are you sure you're not talking about your own wants?"

The woman's eyes fly open wide and she looks as though I've physically struck her. "Just because you're engaged to him doesn't mean he's going to stick with you. He just needs to get women like you out of his system so he can realize who he really needs at his side."

"That will be a great conversation for us to have then, won't it?" I say, adding some sugar to my voice. I might not be convinced Miles would ever see a future with me, but I won't let this woman win with all her hate.

"You'll stay away from him after tonight, do you hear me?"

I'm not sure where it comes from, probably from the stress of seeing Miles deck Clay several days ago and then losing my job, but all I can do is laugh. "I'm sorry, ma'am, but we're both adults and we can figure out what the future will be. Your son is the most amazing guy I've ever met, and he's given me no indication that he's the kind to up and leave when he's made commitments. I don't know what the history is between the two of you or between you and his ex-girlfriends, but I hope you know what you're doing when you try to destroy his relationships behind his back. Because chances are, you're destroying his trust in you."

Shock is the only expression left on the woman's face.

"I might not be high society, but I love Miles Clark. He's nothing like I thought he'd be and everything I could ever hope to have as a husband. I'm sorry I don't meet your standards, but I'm at a point where I now realize I'm not everyone's favorite dessert. And that's okay. I'm not changing who I am because that's what you want."

I turn in the most dramatic way possible, mostly because of the gown I'm wearing and head back toward the doors. Spencer is leaning against one with his phone out.

"Um, I don't know what that was back there, but you could win an award for that acting performance." Spencer points back to where we just left.

"Well, Spencer, I think the trick of that scene was that it was one hundred percent real. Miles is one of those people you meet once in a lifetime and are changed for the better."

"I think he could say the same thing about you."

The encounter leaves me a bit exhausted and I say, "How about we go get something to eat? Maybe that will help me calm down a bit." I glance down at my hands, which are trembling at my sides.

Spencer nods, guiding me to the table. "What do you want to happen after tonight?"

I laugh and shake it off. "Well, a full twelve hours of sleep would be nice."

He pauses and stares at me. "While I applaud that much sleep, I mean between you and Miles."

After blinking several times, my brain finally catches up on the fact that he's asking about my feelings for Miles.

"Is this an investigation like in high school where someone sends their friend to see if their crush likes them back?"

Spencer shrugs. "I never went to high school, so I'm not sure about that. Being a child actor had its perks and disadvantages."

The slight rise of optimism sinks back down. "Honestly, I don't know. I mean, from the display from his mother, it's pretty clear a relationship with Miles wouldn't ever happen."

"Why not? She's just mad because she can't control him anymore."

I take his words and mull them over a bit. "Well, I don't know how well this fake relationship thing is actually going. I mean, it's not like we've had groundbreaking things happen."

Spencer laughs. "I think you're comparing your experience to the movies, Dani. Think about it. Miles decked your ex-boyfriend. His mom came up and tried to split you up. Those are pretty significant, I'd say."

I take a plate and stand behind Spencer in line. But how do I figure out what's real and what's fake? The kisses we've shared have been analyzed to the max by my brain and I still can't figure out what they all mean.

"Hey," Miles says, coming up next to me. He places his hand on my lower back, leaning down to give me a quick peck on the lips. And that just sends me into the confusion spiral of a lifetime. "Sorry I took so long. Those guys wanted to chat about the new research we're doing and I couldn't get away fast enough."

"Did you figure out what you needed from them?" I hope he doesn't ruin any chances by running over to me. Except inwardly I'm kind of excited about it.

"Yeah, we should be good."

CHAPTER 35
Miles

I find Dani in line for food, with Spencer a step behind. The guy is a great friend, and I'm grateful to him for keeping her company.

But he's trying to signal something with his eyes, opening them wide and then pointing toward Dani.

"What's up?" I ask, wondering why he's being so weird.

"Nothing. I'll tell you later."

It's hard to speak with Dani since the room is loud and everyone keeps coming up to say a quick word. If only I could have a sign to hold up for moments like this when I want to be left alone.

We head over to a table near the stage where the band is playing, as that's where I'm usually assigned when my mother is in charge. But tonight I'd rather be on the outskirts so Dani and I can talk.

I pull her seat out and make sure she's sitting comfortably before taking my place next to her.

"How are you?" I ask, trying to catch her eyes. They're the best source to know how she's feeling and from the tense set of her shoulders, I need to fix whatever happened.

"I'm here," she says, turning to me with a smile. It's not the bright kind I'm used to seeing from her.

Resting my hand on the back of her chair, I lean closer, hoping to give her enough space to speak. "I'm so sorry I left you. What can I do to—"

Dani raises her hand, cutting me off. "Miles, you're fine. I know this is work for you. And I'm here to help, just like before."

Something in her eyes comes through as a warning, and I turn toward my plate.

The vibration of my phone causes me to pull it out of my suit coat and I glance down to see a text from Spencer.

Spencer: Your mom talked to her in the hallway.

My stomach turns to lead and I glance up, finding Spencer to see it confirmed on his face. He's sitting at the next table over, giving me a small smile.

I turn toward Dani, noting all the bodily clues that I usually feel after an altercation with my mother.

"Dani," I say, reaching over and taking her hand in mine. She turns to me, surprised.

"Are you all right, Miles?" She turns to check, glancing up and down as if she'll see some outside wound.

"I'm fine. Are you? Did my mom come talk to you?" I hold my breath, not sure what answer I want her to give.

She nods, glancing down at her plate. "Yeah, she told me to stay away from you." When she looks up again, her smile looks drawn on.

"What did you say?" I ask, wishing I could go back and avoid leaving her for even a minute.

Dani opens her mouth to speak, but glances behind me. "It seems like our exes have impeccable timing."

I frown, unsure what she means by that. But it's the voice that pulls the anger throughout my body.

"Looks like this is where I'm supposed to be tonight." Tanya.

Without letting go of Dani's hand, I turn enough to nod at

Tanya and then look back at my fiancé. "Just know, Dani, that no matter what she told you, know that I don't share her opinions."

Dani's smile is somewhat bigger this time and she squeezes my hand. She picks up her fork and starts eating. For some reason, it makes me think of the first time we met all those weeks ago.

"A girl's got to eat, right?" she says and I laugh.

I face forward and start eating some of the food on my plate.

"It sounds like your new girlfriend is causing you to be in the headlines a lot more than before, Miles." Tanya's prim smile as she unfolds her napkin makes me grind my teeth together. "Maybe I should've done that sooner and we'd still be together."

I shake my head. "I don't think that's something I want to give thought to. You ended things and I've never been more grateful than I have these past few weeks. Why are you here?"

Tanya grins, and I don't like what that might mean. "You'll see."

I glance over at Dani, who is focused on her food but I know she's been able to hear the entire conversation.

There's a tap on the microphone behind me and I have to turn in my chair to see what's going on now. The event planner stands there, smiling at the crowd.

"We want to welcome all of you here to the Clark Medical Group Annual Ball. The hostess of tonight would like to make a few announcements before we get started with the full festivities."

My mother walks over and takes the microphone from the woman, putting on her winning smile, the one she pulls out for special occasions.

"Thank you, Ziya. Isn't this place lovely tonight?" Mom says, gesturing to the large room and waiting for applause. Once it dies down, she continues. "We have a lot to be thankful for at the Clark Medical Group. We've been given so many great new hires and a lot of talent to help us help the medical community."

I frown, trying to figure out what she means by all the new hires. She's never cared about them before. People tend to be collateral damage when it comes to Anita Clark.

Slight pressure on my arm causes me to face Dani.

"Breathe. You need to breathe, Miles." With her warning, I recognize the burn in my lungs.

Taking in deep breaths, my heart rate slowly returns to normal. I've missed some of what my mother has said in the process but from where I pick back up, I'm guessing she's started a new tradition of giving out awards. Is this her trying to turn over a new leaf?

"Todd Zundel, for helping expand the current sales department. And Aliyah Reynolds, for her work on the research team for some exciting new advancements we hope to release within the coming year."

Why does all of this sound fake?

Even the people receiving the awards seem surprised.

"And for an announcement that our investors will be excited to learn. A new hire for our company." She pauses a moment. I have to give it to her. She knows how to work a crowd when she wants to.

A new hire? Why would a lower level employee be announced in front of a room of employees, investors, and clients of our company?

"It's with great pleasure that we bring back Tanya Mitchell into the spot of Vice President of Operations. Her time away for the past six months has given her significant experience that will only add to our strength."

I whirl around to face Tanya, my anger from earlier turning to fury. As part owner of the company, I have to have the chance to sign off on any new hires, especially ones that will be working with me on a daily basis.

Shaking my head, I try to keep my voice down once Tanya sits back in her seat. "What's your game? Why come back?"

Tanya smiles. "It's the same game I've been working on for the past four years, Miles. And now I can get everything I want."

My mother finally concludes and walks off the stage. I've got to figure this out and now.

"Dani," I say, folding my napkin and resting it on the table. "I need to speak to my mother about a few things. Will you be all right?"

She nods, her eyes unreadable. "Go. Do what you need to."

I dash out, hoping to get this resolved once and for all. Dani has my heart and no amount of finagling is going to help my mother change my mind.

CHAPTER 36

Dani

Sitting here at a table with Miles's ex is not high on my priority list. Then again, he'd had a conversation with Clay a week ago. Two actually. One with his words and another with his fist.

"How are you settling into the crowd here?" Tanya asks. Something about her has my defenses rising. Obviously having her reinstated to the Clark Medical Group did something to rile up my fiancé. Fake fiancé.

I'd meant to tell him how much I want things between us to continue, but after everything tonight, it might be better to wait.

"I'm learning the ropes," I say, picking up my glass of water.

"That's more than some are willing to do. This crowd, these kind of people can be so intimidating if you don't know exactly what you want and the way to get it."

I tilt my head an inch, trying to read her better. There's a lot of outward confidence, but does that extend inward as well?

"I can understand that. We're all lost if we don't know what we want, right?" I say, using my fork to make a straight line with the rice on my plate.

Tanya leans over, her eyes boring through me. "And what is it you want, Danielle? With all the trouble you've managed to stir up, I would think you'd want to give Miles some space. Less stress about his personal life when he's got enough to worry about at work."

A small measure of doubt enters my brain. And instead of answering, I figure I might as well keep the woman talking. "You're the one who gave him up before. Why come back now?"

She grins and while I'm don't usually resort to violence unless necessary, my fists ball at my sides.

"Because I wanted this position and everything that comes with it."

"And that was worth giving up Miles?"

With a quick shrug, she says, "I doubt it will be long before I have him back." The challenge in her eyes drives that doubt in a bit further and I nod.

"I think you've burned a few too many bridges in your quest to have it all. But that's not my decision."

I stand, taking my clutch with me. "Excuse me. I need to find the Ladies' room."

Without a backward glance, I make my way for the doors to the outside. This room, with all the space for the vaulted ceiling, is too small for me at the moment.

CHAPTER 37
Miles

My mother sees me coming and heads toward a table, greeting them as warmly as she knows how.

I wait a few moments, knowing that all of this is like a game of chess, working to see the angles and the way that I might come through and get the answers I need.

She tries to continue the small talk with the table, but it's awkward and I step forward, flashing a smile to the table. "May I borrow my mother for a minute?"

I wave for her to follow me toward the hall, and we make it out into an area where I can actually think.

"What is going on? Since when are we bringing Tanya back? I should've been notified."

My mother's chin tips up a bit, showing the defiance in her eyes. "You've been too busy with your pretend fiancé to take much notice in the company. This is something that needs to happen, Miles."

"Our relationship isn't pretend, Mom," I say, hope infusing my words. "We work together well, and I enjoy spending time with her. I love her, Mom."

She shakes her head, frustration etched into her features. "You don't know what love is. Love is something that can turn your whole world upside down with one diagnosis. It's something that is only known by fools."

My stomach constricts and I have to choke out the words, "Are you saying you weren't a fool? That you didn't love Dad?"

"What we had was different."

"How do you know, Mom? You've barely spoken to Dani and, from everything I've heard, it was to try and warn her away from me."

My words are more as a test than actual knowledge, but she doesn't deny it.

"You'll be better off with Tanya. You'll be the next power couple of Boston. And think of how far you two can take this company in the next several decades. Something to pass down to your children."

It's then that my mind comes up with a different future. Not one filled with only meetings and mergers, but one with laughter and fun. Of course, work will have to be part of it, but I can't continue like this.

Work that will help to ease the suffering of others.

"I quit."

That seems to have gotten through to my mother. "What?"

"I'm done. Tell Tanya she can buy out my share of the company if she wants. I no longer want to play this game."

"You can't quit. You're the namesake of this company. Everything your father and I built was for you."

I nod. "I appreciate that mother, but you haven't stopped trying to build my life even now. I have a brain that functions, that can make decisions that are right for me. And right now, my decision is to walk away and be with the woman I love."

Without another word, I run back toward the party, panicking when I see Dani's seat is empty.

I charge over to the table and glare at Tanya. "Where is Dani?"

"She might've gone to the ladies' room. Or maybe she decided to head home. Shouldn't you know what she'd do, as her fiancé that is?" Her words are a challenge, but my mind has lumped her in with my mother, people who can work together while I pursue my own path.

I try to be as casual as possible walking through the large room in the direction of one of the restrooms. Why would Dani leave?

Does she think this is what I want?

When a woman walks out of the restroom, I call, "Dani! Dani!" inside. There's no response. I push the door open a bit, grateful for the wall that blocks everything on the other side. I don't need people thinking I'm crazy.

"Dani, are you in here?"

"Miles, what's wrong?" Dani's voice asks from behind me. I turn, grateful to see her standing there.

In a swift move, I bridge the gap between us and pull her into my arms. I pull back enough to lean down and kiss her, the action making chills run throughout my body.

I deepen the kiss, wrapping my arms around her waist and tugging her closer. It's possible it's just in my head, but she's relaxed in my arms, her hands reaching up and twirling the longer sections of hair near my neck.

And then she goes rigid, as if she's just realized something.

She steps back, nearly out of my grasp. Glancing around the hallway, she blushes as she sees a woman who must have been watching the show.

Dani steps forward and takes my hand. "That was some good acting, Señor Miles."

I shake my head. "No acting needed."

Her gaze shoots up to my eyes. "What do you mean?"

Blowing out a breath, I lead her into an alcove down the hall from the restrooms. This is one conversation I want without anyone interrupting.

"Dani, this all started out fake because I was too chicken to stand up to my mother about running my own life." Her smile falls and she glances away. I take my fingers and softly turn her chin to look back at me. "This arrangement we've had is something I've never been more grateful for. I've had some toxic people in my life and you were there when I needed you most."

"W-what are you saying?" Dani stutters.

"Dani, I'm saying that somehow, in the craziness of the past couple months, you've managed to show me that life can be different. Wonderful and fun. That I need laughter and love, the kind I get from you."

She's got her mouth open slightly and I want to kiss her again. Instead, I hold back, knowing I need to get this out before her kisses make my brain go haywire again.

"I quit, Dani."

She blinks several times and says, "Wait, what? You quit our relationship?"

I hold onto her hands again and say, "No, I never want that to happen. I quit the company."

"Are you okay? What happened?" Dani says, letting go of one hand to reach up and press it against my cheek.

"Well, I'm going to finish out the project with Oliver. And work on a few other projects that will help the medical community on its lower levels. I won't be earning a ton at the beginning, but if you're willing to stick with me through it, I know anything can happen."

I step forward, feeling excited about the fact that I've finally been able to tell her all that. What I want most now is a kiss.

Instead, Dani places a hand on my chest to stop me. "Wait, let me rewind that a bit in my head. First of all, you said you don't want to stop our relationship and then you want me to be with you after that? Are you trying to give me a job?" There's a slight smile at the corner of her lips and the panic eases in my chest.

"Dani, I love you. I've never met someone so strong. After everything you've gone through and everything I've put you through, I was scared to tell you how I feel. Nervous that I'd be stuck in the friend zone after this weekend."

She raises her eyebrows and grins. "You? Worried about the

friend zone?" Her laugh fills the air of the small space and she grabs onto my lapels and pulls me in for a kiss.

What seems like minutes later, we pull back and I ask, "So is that a yes or a no to the friend zone?"

She laughs and shakes her head. "Miles, I have loved you since game night with my family. So that's a no to friend zone and a yes to whatever step we're supposed to be on in this relationship."

I run a hand through my hair and laugh. "We've done a lot of things all backward, haven't we?"

"I don't know if it would've worked any other way," Dani says, her voice softer than before. She lifts her left hand and pulls the ring off. "Here."

I take it from her and put it right back on her left hand. "This is right where it needs to be. On the ring finger of the woman I love."

Dani blinks several times as tears form. "I love you, too, Miles."

"Do we need Dr Pepper to seal the deal this time?" I grin, marveling at how much my life has changed in a few short weeks since we met.

Shaking her head, Dani jabs me in the shoulder. "Really? Is that going to be a running joke our entire lives?"

I nod. "I doubt anyone can top it."

Epilogue

Dani

Never would I have thought, after breaking up with Clay, that I'd be graduating from college and getting married in the same year.

Miles renewed his proposal at The Riptide, where Dr Pepper wasn't allowed at any of the tables nearby, per my request.

We were married at a fun little place in Carlisle, and we've been on our honeymoon in Europe for the past week.

"Okay, so what do we need to check off for the honeymoon bucket list?" Miles asks, pulling out a blank sheet of paper. "We've seen Big Ben and you've had your fill of crepes from France. You did not meet your goal of eating your weight in them, but avoiding a trip to the hospital is always a good idea."

I pause, retracing memories as I try to remember where he got that notion. "I said that?"

He nods and laughs. "The day I proposed our fake relationship."

Lightbulbs go off and I smile, pulling him in for a lengthy kiss. Something I will never get tired of.

"How did you remember something like that?"

"I don't know what kind of magical power you have, but I remember a lot of the things you say." He grins and I still can't believe this is my life.

I smile and say, "Well, in a couple months, you'll need to remember to pick up your socks and clean the mirror after brushing your teeth, or whatever it is married couples fight about."

"I think we can arrange that." He leans forward and pulls me in for another kiss. "You make it hard to get out of bed, Dani-girl."

"Well, unlike some people in this room," I say, giving him a pointed look, "I've never seen Prague. And we don't want to keep Oliver forever."

Nodding, Miles walks over to the bathroom and turns on the shower.

The few weeks after Miles left the family company had been stressful for both of us, but getting things finished up for the launch of the machines to hospitals in September had been worth it. Miles and Oliver had started their own company, combining the best of both worlds with their separate expertise.

Am I complaining about extending our honeymoon for business purposes in Europe? No, no I'm not.

As the public relations specialist for the new company, this is something I can get behind.

"I can't believe I'm here," I say, taking in the beauty of the city.

Miles nods. "Yeah, imagine what would've happened if I'd asked the woman from that dating app to be my fake girlfriend." He pauses for a moment and then says, "Oh wait, I did."

After several lengthy conversations over the course of our real engagement, we figured out that he wasn't the creepy guy living in his parents' basement I'd originally thought. Not that I needed the help of a matchmaking app to tell me Miles and I would work, but it definitely makes me smile.

Once we're both dressed and ready, Miles turns to me and

asks, "Should we shop at the markets first, or go see the Prague Castle?"

"We're supposed to be meeting with Oliver." I give him a look that is supposed to be stern, but it's difficult when I realize all that my life has turned out to be.

"We can meet and see the sights."

I shake my head. "Which usually means we'll talk about business for five minutes and spend the rest of the time among the tourists."

"That's not a bad thing, love. Work will always be there, but we won't always be here."

He leans in for a kiss before we walk out of the hotel and into the Prague sunshine.

A year ago I thought I knew what I wanted my life to be. And somehow in the twists and turns, it's heads and tails better than I could've imagined.

About the Author

By day, Britney M. Mills is the wife to a builder and mom to five, but by night, she turns into an author, writing YA & contemporary romance stories.

A book lover, former college athlete, and Jane Austen fan, she crafts stories with the idea that anyone can find love.

When she's not writing, she spends time playing games with her kids, or shuttling them to and from their activities, watching Sanditon and Murdock Mysteries, or dreaming of future characters while she folds a mountain of laundry.

Subscribe to Britney's newsletter for updates, behind-the-scenes and a free book to dive into today!

Acknowledgments

With every book, I'm not the only person working on it.

I'm grateful for my amazing beta readers. They put up with the rough draft and gave me all the tips to refine the story. To Nina, for your patience on all the half-drafts I sent. You're amazing.

To Amy Sparling for being an amazing proofreader. I appreciate you more than you know.

To Sheree, my amazing VA, you're awesome and thanks for keeping things going when I drop all the things.

And to my husband and kids, for sometimes allowing me to work on this. :) I'm grateful for the support system I have at home, and for them surviving through the mound of clothes I've neglected to fold.

Also by Britney M. Mills

Romance by Love, Austen

Matched with Her Runaway Groom

Love Austen Series

Love, Austen

Austen, Party of Two

Austen Unscripted

Matched, Austen

Austen, Edited

Testing Love, Austen

International Billionaire Club

The Australian Billionaire

The French Billionaire

The British Billionaire

The Vegas Billionaire

The Italian Billionaire

Christmas at Coldwater Creek

Love in a Blizzard

Love in the Lights

Love in a Snapshot

Love in the Details

Rosemont High Baseball

The Perfect Play

The Perfect Game

The Perfect Catch

The Perfect Steal

The Perfect Hit

Sage Creek Small Town Series

Loving His Flower Shop Girl

Loving His Reporter Girl

Subscribe to the newsletter to get updates on books coming out, cover reveals and the opportunity for giveaways!

www.ingramcontent.com/pod-product-compliance
Lightning Source LLC
Chambersburg PA
CBHW030114260626
47156CB00008B/2655